TRUE STORIES

OF THE WILD WEST

Michel Lipman
and
Cathy Furniss

A Bluewood Book

Train Crosses Canyon Diablo, AZ - 1883

This edition produced and published in 1998 by Bluewood Books
A Division of The Siyeh Group, Inc.
P.O. Box 689
San Mateo, CA 94401

ISBN 0-912517-29-8

Printed in U.S.A.
10, 9, 8, 7, 6, 5, 4, 3, 2, 1

Edited by: Holly Blumenthal, Heidi Marschner and Colleen Turrell
Proofread by: Nancy Hamilton
Design and Production by: David Price

About the Authors:

MICHEL LIPMAN
A Freedom Foundation award-winner, he is the creator of the long-running
syndicated radio show "Point of Law" and author of dozens of books and
articles on a variety of subjects. Mr. Lipman resides in San Francisco, CA.

CATHY FURNISS
Ms. Furniss also resides in San Francisco, CA and has written numerous books
on subjects ranging from fine arts, theater and music. As a child actress, she
worked in over 150 Hollywood movies, many of them were about the West.

ACKNOWLEDGEMENTS

For the authors, this has been a labor of love. We've been fascinated by our dips into the past and our meetings with people of an earlier time. Not the least of the pleasure has been in the help, inspiration and encouragement of the following people and organizations, who we are happy to acknowledge and thank:

The California Historical Society, the Victorian Alliance of San Francisco, the Nevada County Historical Society, the Wells Fargo Historical Museum and Library, Tom and Mimi Winston, David Adams, Lynn Brandon, Ann Bloomfield, Susan Scott, and the wonderful people at the San Francisco Public Library.

The publisher wishes to thank and acknowledge the following for the courtesy of reproducing the following images:

Bluewood Books Archives: 28, 42, 44, 65, 76, 106; Buffalo Bill Historical Center, Cody, WY: 57, 140; California State Library: 113; George Eastman House: 31; Library of Congress: cover, 13, 16, 19, 23, 36, 51, 69, 78, 81, 83, 99, 103, 104, 120, 123, 129, 133; National Archives: cover, 2, 9, 11, 33, 55, 59, 63, 67, 91, 95, 109, 111, 117, 127; New Mexico, Museum of: 137; San Jose Historical Museum: 47; Texas State Library: 115; Union Pacific Railroad: 21; U.S. Dept. of Interior: cover, 71, 87; Western History Collections; University of Oklahoma Library: 25

DEDICATION

To all dreamers
of the impossible dream,
especially the Victorian Alliance,
for working to save
what is meaningful and elegant
from our past.

TABLE OF CONTENTS

Langtry, TX - Judge Roy Bean's Office, 1900

INTRODUCTION

ack in the 1850s, there was a great rush of people to the western United States. Some intended to find gold mines and become rich. Others — many others — came for different reasons. And those reasons, even for professional historians, remain a mystery. Some of the historians wonder if people came west because they thought the United States really was a land of boundless opportunities. Other historians think the rush was due to industrialization — the growth of factories and mass production that led to ever more crowded cities. Still others look at the floods of immigrants from abroad and the subsequent class conflicts — rich against poor, labor against capital — as the cause of the mass resettlement.

Surely there is merit in some of these theories. Probably the answer lies in a combination of them. In any event, *something* sent huge numbers of eager Americans westward. They traveled by covered wagon, by long voyage around the southern tip of South America, or across the steamy, malaria-ridden Isthmus of Panama.

No one, it seems, ever turned back. These pioneers put up with unbelievable hardship and faced enormous dangers, including hostile natives, heartless bandits, unforgiving storms and strength-sapping heat. There were breakdowns, runaway oxen, impassable routes, incompetent guides and illness. For many, there was death on the trail. But still they came. They were innovative, self-reliant and confident. If they didn't have what they needed, they built it. If it didn't exist, they invented it.

The men fixed broken equipment with whatever material they could find. They improvised and made do. In their spare time they fought with the Native Americans, doctored sick animals and hunted wild game to add to their staples of dried beans and moldy flour. The women were equally hardy: They tended the

Harry Yount Was The First Ranger In Yellowstone National Park

children, cooked every meal, loaded the single-shot rifles during attacks and occasionally did some shooting on their own.

These pioneers must have had huge expectations for reward to risk their very beings on such a journey. A powerful lure was drawing them in.

But what was it?

One landmark historian dug deep — and came up with an idea that changed the whole focus of the theories about western settlement. Frederick Jackson Turner proposed that the promise of a special kind of wealth — ownership of land — was the lure. Turner saw that the best lands on the Eastern Seaboard had already been taken up by earlier pioneers in the 1600s, 1700s and early 1800s.

At least half of the U.S. population by that time was farmers, or sons and daughters of farmers, who wanted farms of their own. But land prices were high, and when a man borrowed money to buy a farm — if he was lucky enough to find a lender for the money — his interest payments on the loan usually ate up any profits he could make. As a result few would-be farmers could afford enough land to feed and house their families.

Turner looked at the huge migration from the East as one solution to an evolving need. As more and more land was claimed and farmed, later immigrants had to look further and further west for acreage they could afford.

Turner's theory had its critics, but other historians took a more careful look — they used the tools of economics, sociology, political science and social psychology. They did some in-depth studies of pioneer communities. In the words of Professor Ray Billington, "They agreed ... that the West did serve as a 'safety valve' [and] lessened social pressures along the seaboard." Professor Billington recognized that the migratory instinct was so deep-seated in the United States that it altered social behavior, just as Turner had said.

Even though the discovery of gold in California was a magnet that drew a large population in a very short time, it seems that growth would have continued anyway.

But whatever reasons they had for coming west, those who came made up a multifaceted group. "Diversity" wasn't a popular term back then, but there certainly was plenty of it. People came to the Western Frontier from Germany, Mexico, Central America, South America, Asia, India, Ireland and Italy. They also came from countries like Bohemia, Prussia, Herzegovina, Bavaria, the Sandwich Islands and other places with names that no longer appear on the map.

John Fremont In Front Of The Giant Tree

They were people of many skills, temperaments, backgrounds, professions and ambitions. There were talented painters, photographers, historians, novelists, teachers, journalists and soldiers, and they have left us valuable records and pictures of western life in past decades. We even have some of the journals and diaries of a variety of people, which tell us of farming life, of cattle drives and of insect infestations in their orchards and fields, as well as more generally of their trials, disappointments and triumphs.

In *True Stories of the Wild West*, you will find a colorful cross-section of these people, from a Chinese monk who visited here in the year A.D. 499, to an intrepid early aviator who flew a Wright Brothers biplane in the first cross-country flight to the Pacific Ocean.

Every story has a historic basis: The events really happened. We have tried to tell them in a style consistent with the times, and we hope not without a touch of humor. **TS**

GREELEY GOES WEST

Horace Greeley was the famous publisher who said, "Go west, young man, go west" — but he didn't really know how hard that was until he tried it himself.

It was a lovely spring day in 1859 when Greeley reached Manhattan, Kansas. That was about as far west as you could go by rail in those days; the rest of the way you had to travel by stage. However, Greeley discovered that this so-called stage was really a "mud wagon" drawn by mules. These conveyances always traveled in pairs so one could help the other in the likely event that it got stuck on the muddy trails. No matter; Greeley grabbed his suitcase and joined the other passengers, and the mules plodded off.

Greeley had been told there would be way stations across the 575 miles of wild prairie. He pictured that they would be like train stations, but these actually turned out to be leaky, badly stocked tents. He was not a man to grumble, but Greeley did ask the wagon master why they couldn't travel some at night to make better time. The wagon master probably just chewed his plug of tobacco for a few moments and then replied, "Could be so, Mr. Greeley, except we might get run over by a herd of stampeding buffalo. I mean, you've never seen such herds, Mr. Greeley. So many as to darken the earth." Greeley didn't argue and, being fond of clever language, jotted down the wagon master's expression to use later in his writing.

All in all, Greeley was a good sport. The meals were not epicurean; Greeley must have had an iron stomach, for he was the only passenger who enjoyed them. And his spirits stayed high, even though he lost his trunk after two of the mules fell at a water crossing.

Mules cannot be made to hurry, so the pace was slow past Denver, around the Great Salt Lake Desert, and over the awful Cortez Mountains to Carson City, Nevada. From here

Horace Greeley

they advanced only 50 miles a day. The final lap down the Sierras, however, was a fast one. They clattered and bounced down the slopes, around high cliffs and narrow canyons. The passengers were bumped and jostled against the roof, the sides and each other. Finally, covered with dust, they plodded into Placerville, California.

The shaken but undaunted publisher wrote back to his paper, "I cannot conscientiously recommend the route to summer tourists in search of pleasure, but it is balm for my many bruises to know that I am at last in CALIFORNIA!" **TS**

WILDERNESS EXPLORER

On tip-toe she stood barely five feet tall and, when loaded down with the bulky clothing of the 1870s, she weighed barely 100 pounds. Few would have marked this 40-year-old spinster to become a famous wilderness explorer — but that's exactly what Isabella Bird went and did.

It was perhaps a combination of her restless spirit and the predictability of her home on the Scottish Isle of Mull that prompted Isabella to leave for a life of adventure. She became a missionary and spent a year in New Zealand, then six months on the Sandwich Islands, eventually making her way to Hawaii. From there she wrote with shocked delight to her sister back in Mull, "It is a wonderful place, and the women here ride their horses astride, not sidesaddle like proper Englishwomen."

While she traveled, Isabella wrote many letters and even wrote books. By age 25 she had published a fascinating book entitled *The English Woman in America*. And yet sometimes she yearned for a different kind of life.

One of her trips led her to Colorado Springs and then on to a secret valley called Estes Park, where she met a huge, hulking trapper named Mountain Jim. He was a hard-drinking, tough-fighting character, one-eyed and disfigured from a battle with a bear. Yet as Isabella wrote her sister, "His manner was chivalrous, his accent refined, and his language easy and elegant." The rough mountain man and the adventurous Scottish lady fell in love, but, as a missionary dedicated to travel, Isabella felt that marriage was impossible and she and Jim parted as friends.

Not long afterward, Jim was shot to death by another man in a fight over some land. By that time, Isabella was in Switzerland, and she wrote to her sister that she saw Jim's spirit in a vision on that day. She seemed to have a change of heart about marriage after that. When her sister's doctor courted her for two years, she finally agreed to marry him. However, she didn't give up her travels, and at age 61 she became the first woman member of England's Royal Geographical Society.

Isabella died at the age of 72, just after crossing the Atlas Mountains of North Africa on a horse belonging to the Sultan of Morocco. But her story lives on through her many books that tell of her travels and missionary work in Kashmir, Seoul and on the Yangtse river, as well as her adventures in Hawaii, the Malayas, India, Turkistan and China. She published such titles as *Chinese Pictures* and *Journeys in Persia and Kurdistan*. In fact her best-seller, *A Lady's Life in the Rocky Mountains*, is still read with pleasure today. **TS**

FLYING WEST

Getting to California from the East wasn't easy back in the 1800s and early 1900s — not by covered wagon, nor on a balky steam train, nor by trekking across the jungles of the Isthmus of Panama. The trip was *definitely* not easy by airplane.

The Wright brothers flew their first fragile biplane in 1903 — for a whopping distance of just 120 feet. Eight years later, millionaire William Randolph Hearst offered $50,000 in prize money to the first person to fly coast to coast in 30 days or less. Although three pilots attempted the feat, two dropped out early on, and only one actually made it from New York to Pasadena, California. He was a tough, six-foot-four cigar-chomping race-car driver turned flyer; his name was Calbraith Perry Rodgers.

Before the attempt, Rodgers met with reporters to answer questions. He showed off the

Vin Fiz, his B Model Wright Brothers biplane powered by a four cylinder, 35-horse motor, with a full-out top speed of 60 miles an hour. He told the reporters he figured on 20 flying days, at an average of 175 miles a day or better. Then on September 17, 1911, he took off from Sheepshead Bay, New York, and soared half a mile up over Manhattan before turning westward.

Wright Flyer Biplane

He located his escort train on the Erie Company railroad tracks and began the long trek across the country. This train carried his mechanics, some spare parts, a second airplane, his wife and his mother. Rodgers first landed at Middletown, New York, where 9,000 people gathered to see him. He came in for a perfect landing: "Didn't even knock the ash off my cigar," he remarked to the welcoming committee. "It's Chicago now in four days."

Things didn't go quite as he had planned. Taking off from Middletown, Rodgers scraped his plane's undercarriage against a tree, slowing his ascent so much that he failed to clear the power lines ahead of him. The plane caught on the lines and flipped over into a chicken coop. Rodgers climbed out of the wreck with his head bleeding — but still holding on to a cigar. "Anybody got a match?" he asked. It took the mechanics 40 hours to patch up the plane. Rodgers wouldn't reach Chicago until 20 days later.

The next leg of the trip went fine, until a defective spark plug popped out. Rodgers managed to land, damaging only his right skid, but he had to wait for his train and the mechanics.

Those problems were just the beginning, however. Rodgers suffered through 16 major and near-fatal crashes during the rest of the trip. While flying over Imperial Junction, California, the plane's engine exploded and Rodgers was seriously injured by shards of flying metal. Between Pasadena and Long Beach, he suffered another major crash that left him with internal injuries and a broken ankle. But nothing stopped him.

On December 10, 1911, with his leg in a cast and his crutches tied to the side of the plane, Rodgers stepped into the *Vin Fiz* yet again. By this time, everything had been rebuilt so many times after so many crashes that none of the parts remained from the original plane except for the rudder, the engine drip pan, and one small piece of the structural support. But the plane was still going strong, and Rodgers flew her up and over the Pacific Ocean and dove down in celebration, gently dipping her wheels into the foaming surf.

Afterward, having won the transcontinental race, Rodgers said modestly, "My record will not stand long. With proper landing places the trip can easily be made in 30 days or less." As we well know today, the persistent adventurer was right. **TS**

CRAZY JUDAH

Back in the 1850s, they called him "Crazy" Judah. Little did they know he would prove them wrong and win fame by solving a so-called impossible problem. Still, his success would only make others rich.

The skeptics had been saying that nobody could build a railroad across the terrible mountains that divided the American West. Theodore Judah didn't believe them. He was a highly skilled engineer and a man of great integrity. He made a preliminary study of the mountains and decided that a railroad line at Dutch Flat would open a practical route through the forbidding Sierra Nevada mountains.

But you can't build much — let alone an entire railroad — without money. Judah lobbied for government support for building such an important new railroad line linking the East and the West. Eventually he found some merchants

Theodore Judah

from Sacramento, California, willing to invest in his company, named the Central Pacific Railroad Company. And he got his government subsidy.

Westerners made him a hero, but his four investors had other ideas. *They* wanted to control the company — and the extra money it was getting from the government to build the route. They threatened to back out of the deal unless he would agree to accept $100,000 as payment for his interest in the project, a deal that would leave him with no say in company decisions.

Judah was furious. "I'm going to New York, to raise capital there," he said. "And *then* we'll see who runs my company!" He took off for New York, but on the way he contracted yellow fever. He died shortly before his 38th birthday.

The investors did complete the railroad. Passengers in 1869 could ride from Omaha, Nebraska to San Francisco, California — a run of almost 2,000 miles — in less than a week. In those days, before income tax, the investors all became rich beyond their wildest dreams.

Despite their good fortune, however, they never shared a dollar of those riches with Judah's widow.

The names of the Big Four investors are still well-known throughout the West – Leland Stanford, Charles Crocker, Collis Huntington and Mark Hopkins. Judah himself is hardly remembered. There is, however, a San Francisco street named after him, and these days you can ride the Judah Street streetcar all the way across town, from the edge of the Pacific Ocean to the shore of the San Francisco Bay. **TS**

THE CROOKED POLICEMAN AND THE MERCIFUL SHERIFF

Small Town Sheriff

Justice in the early West was quick and tough. If you killed, you got a judge-and-jury trial — and were promptly hanged. Even for a brutal killer, though, there could sometimes be a glimmer of mercy.

Such a thing happened in Penascal, Texas, in 1874. Three bodies were found there on a Sunday morning. A cook, who had survived the raid on the town's only store, said there had been 10 or 11 raiders. They'd taken goods and the few dollars in the store's till and escaped in a wagon.

A posse formed, and the posse leader figured the killers were heading for Mexico, 100 miles to the south. But one of the posse members noticed some brown powder on the ground near the crime scene. He wetted a finger and tasted it gingerly — it was brown sugar! The trail of sugar ran *north*, toward Corpus Christi. The posse followed it and soon found two of the raiders hiding among a group of sheep shearers.

The raiders claimed the raid had been planned by a member of the city's police force, one Tomás Basquez. Basquez had it all set up — he knew when a boatload of supplies and money was scheduled to land at Penascal, and he had gathered a strike force of thugs to raid the store there after it had stocked up on fresh goods. Things didn't go exactly as planned, though. The thugs struck when they saw the boat out in the bay, figuring it had already come and unloaded its cargo in Penascal, when in fact it hadn't. The raiders got much less than they had planned on in terms of loot.

Basquez was never found, but the two captured raiders were tried and sentenced to be hanged. At first in jail they played cards, joked and laughed, but, as the day of their execution drew near, they realized their fate and became withdrawn and glum. Two days before the hanging, one of the men asked the sheriff for a last wish. The sheriff was hesitant, but he told the man to ask anyway.

The killer told the sheriff about his girl-friend. They had been living together for several years and had three children, he said, but they had never gotten married, and the bandit didn't think it was right. He asked the sheriff to allow them a marriage ceremony.

The sheriff felt that glimmer of mercy. He arranged for decent dress and a shave for the man and sent for a priest. He also put a heavy guard around the jail to discourage a possible rescue attempt. The bride sobbed throughout the ceremony. The sheriff allowed them only one embrace. The next day the two men were hanged.

Police tried for years afterward to find other gang members, but they were unsuccessful. As for their leader, the crooked policeman, he was never seen or heard from again. **TS**

NANA'S STRANGE SECRET

In the Wild West, problems were often resolved with a fist or a gun. However, violence only brings more violence, as is illustrated by the strange fate of the Bandit Queen, Belle Starr.

Belle Starr was straight out of legend — she led a band of cattle rustlers and horse thieves as they did mischief through the Indian Territory, all the while riding in velvet gowns and broad-brimmed feathered hats. It has been a mystery for many years, though: Who murdered Belle Starr?

Belle was 43 when, on February 3, 1889, someone blew her out of the saddle with a shotgun. There were plenty of suspects. One historian claimed that Belle's angry son, Ed Reed, did her in. Others believed it may have been Jim Middleton, the brother of a former lover, or perhaps even Jim July, a Creek Indian who was

Belle Starr

Belle's lover at the time she was killed. Nothing definite has been proven regarding her murder. We can guess, though, that the cattle ranchers and horse breeders in those parts breathed a sigh of relief at her passing.

The years rolled by and Belle was pretty much forgotten — until one family's strange secret came to light. In about 1912, an elderly woman known to her family as Nana Devena swore everyone to secrecy when she finally revealed what she had done. "Her face lit up," recalled her grandson 58 years after she told the story, "and she said, 'I've got something to tell all of you … *I killed Belle Starr*.'"

Devena was born in South Carolina in the 1840s, and by the 1880s she had moved with her husband to a farm near Eufaula, in the region that is now eastern Oklahoma. After her husband died, she had the hard job of raising five children on her own on the frontier, and with little money.

As Devena related the story, she had had a row with some neighbors. The neighbors had objected when Devena allowed her two sons to do some work for another neighbor because they didn't like him. But she had ignored their warnings because the family needed the money. In retaliation, the neighbors had several times turned her milk cows loose during the night and stolen corn from her corncrib. As the feud progressed, a neighbor boy snuck up behind her in the corral and struck her to the ground. He beat and kicked her until her daughter, hearing her screams, ran to the rescue. Devena had had enough.

That very afternoon, Devena loaded up her shotgun and marched up to the road, where she saw the boy on horseback riding toward town. He was too far away at that point, so she waited for his return, standing there until in the darkness she made out a rider coming along the road from the direction of town. She shot the rider, thinking it was her enemy. Before long she heard the news that Belle Starr had been shot and killed along the road. Devena never breathed a word of what she did for many years. **TS**

HARVEY HOUSES

You might have enjoyed taking a steam train across the country in the 1860s, but your stomach definitely wouldn't have. The Santa Fe Railroad passenger train stopped for lunch and dinner but only allowed 20 minutes for each. The food at the rail-side diners — well, "ugh" was an apt description of what you had to choose from. You'd get greasy fried meat, served just before the train was ready to go, or hard-boiled eggs preserved in lime. The hot cup of coffee you'd try to gulp down before your train left would have been brewed more than two days earlier. This state of affairs finally came to change for the better, though, when Fred Harvey and his Harvey Houses arrived on the scene.

Fred Harvey came to America at the age of 15. He worked as a busboy and a pantry man, and he later opened two cafes of his own while working full time for the Chicago-Burlington Railroad as a freight agent. But the C&B wasn't interested in his plan for company restaurants along their lines.

The Santa Fe line, however, did listen. With the company's blessing, the first Harvey House cafe went up in Florence, Kansas. It was a huge success, partly because Santa Fe trains stopped at the door, and partly because Harvey kept to unheard-of high standards of food, service and cleanliness. More Harvey lunchrooms and dining rooms opened along the Santa Fe, becoming an enormous draw for the railroad.

Harvey's employee relations were quite advanced for the times. A Harvey Girl waitress could work her way up to head waitress and a substantial increase in pay; a few waitresses even became managers. These were remarkable opportunities for women in the 1800s, and thousands of young women flocked to join the Harvey organization.

Harvey insisted on the customer-is-always-right approach. If a customer complained to him about one of the managers, Harvey would have called the man in. "Charley," he would have said, "Mr. Conover says you didn't treat him fairly today."

Charley, the manager, might have had an excuse: "Mr. Harvey, that man is in here all the time, and he's a regular crank."

"Charley," would come the reply, "I hired you to please just that kind of person!"

Harvey died in 1901, but his business continued to thrive. In the 1940s, the system was running about 50 restaurants, a dozen major hotels, 100 newsstands and several dozen retail shops. It supervised service on over 100 Santa Fe dining cars. The golden era of Harvey's dining service came to an end after World War II, when the automobile and the airplane brought a decline to rail travel and an end to elegant railroad restaurants. **TS**

The Food At Road-Side Diners Was Terrible

DODGE CITY DOCTOR

He wore a long, formal, black coat and a tall silk hat along with his holstered .45 — but nobody ever laughed because, for all his being barely five feet tall in his boots, Samuel Crumbine was a physician far in advance of his time.

Samuel, whose father died in the Civil War before he was born, worked in a pharmacy to earn money to pay for his medical school tuition. When he had used up all his funds at medical school, he headed west and landed in Dodge City, Kansas. The booming, boisterous town must have appealed to his orphanage-starved sense of adventure because he fell in love with it at first sight.

But it is said you can't live on love alone, and Sam and his new bride were hard-pressed for cash. Many of Sam's patients paid in vegetables, eggs, chicken or salt pork. That was fine in most cases, but the landlord wanted his rent in cash, not cabbages. Then one day Sam got a call from a rancher who lived 35 miles out of town, Jim Fairmore. He'd been tossed from an unbroken bronco.

Doctor Sam rode out and set the man's broken leg. He was about to leave when the patient pulled out a large Colt revolver. "Sorry, Doc, you ain't going nowhere just yet. Maybe tomorrow, when we're sure there ain't no complications." So Sam stayed with the man overnight, and when the patient saw that things were just fine the next morning, he let him go. Later, when Sam got to his office, a messenger came in and delivered a bag of gold as thanks for the doctor's being "a guest at breakfast."

Sam's fortune seemed to change for the better with that generous bonanza. Everyone in town quickly grew to know and respect the pint-sized medical man. He, in turn, used his new-found respect to bring proper health practices into common use and to convince the pharmacies to keep "snake oil" and other ineffective medicines off their shelves. Sam urged famed restaurateur Fred Harvey to stop serving milk in pitchers, since harmful bacteria easily got into the open containers, rapidly multiplying in the milk and possibly making people sick. He insisted that smallpox patients should be vaccinated and allowed to stay home instead of being held together in a disease-breeding public lock-up. His best shot was against the common house-fly, for Sam believed, and rightly so, that there was a link between the flies and typhoid fever. "Swat that fly!" he growled, and folks took his advice to heart.

Sam lived to be 91. Dodge City is nothing like it used to be back then, but Sam's practical health advice is still followed today. **TS**

TOM MAGUIRE'S MANY THEATERS

This is the story of a determined individual named Tom Maguire who persisted with his dream – despite facing setback after setback. With his vision, he brought culture to the West.

In 1849, Tom Maguire was a carriage driver in New York City. Having heard about the prosperous gold mining going on in the West, he and his wife packed up and went to San Francisco, California, to make their own fortune. They opened a saloon at Kearny and Washington Streets and, since there was no shortage of thirsty miners in the fast-growing city, soon built up a large cash surplus.

Tom, who had spent a great deal of time in the New York theatrical area, had a great admiration for theatrical culture. He got to figuring that what those miners really craved was quality entertainment. It so happened that there was a second story to his building — and above his saloon was an open, unoccupied loft. He decided to turn the space into a theater.

On October 30, 1850, Tom opened up the Jenny Lind Theater, named after a famous opera star who had no connection with the theater. The theater was a great success — Tom's inclination had been right. The miners, merchants, builders and shipping workers who cashed in on the gold rush had it all, it would seem, but still they yearned for finer things in life. Described in the newspapers of the time as "high-minded,

Downtown San Francisco, 1850's

pure and virtuous," theater events were regarded as an antidote to the moral depravity and carousing that seemed to prevail in that era.

Tom's financial success with the theater continued until disaster struck: The Jenny Lind Theater burned to the ground on May 4, 1851. But Tom was determined for the theater to continue to prosper in the city, and so he set about building a second Jenny Lind, located where the previous theater had been. The second Jenny Lind opened on June 13. It was more elegant than the first theater had been, and crowds turned out to see the performances for a couple of weeks until the theater once again caught fire and burned down.

Tom was not one to give up easily, and he brushed off this second disaster, building a new theater. The third Jenny Lind opened on October 4, 1851. Within a single year Tom Maguire had built and rebuilt his theater three times! The newest Jenny Lind was the most imposing of the three. In fact, *The Herald* newspaper had announced, "Mr. Thomas Maguire, so often burnt out and as often rising with energies unsubdued by misfortune, is now engaged in constructing a building which will be an ornament to the city."

Although over 2,000 people crowded into the new theater on opening night, the year 1852 found a decreased interest in theater-going. Tom was forced eventually to sell the Jenny Lind. The city of San Francisco bought the building for $200,000 and used it as the City Hall for many years.

With the money Tom made from the sale, he bought a three-story building known as San Francisco Hall. He renamed it Maguire's Opera House, and it turned out to be his most successful theater. Some of the nation's greatest talent performed there. Among the famous actors he engaged were Edwin Booth, John McCullough, Edwin Forrest, Frank Mayo and Adah Isaacs Menken.

By 1858 Tom had opened theaters throughout California — in Sacramento, Stockton, Sonora and several mining centers that have long since become ghost towns. In the 1860s, in order to expose the city to grand opera, he built the Academy of Music on Pine Street in San Francisco. Tom made some bad business guesses later and lost a great deal of money. He went to New York for financing where he eventually died in 1896. But he holds an important place in San Francisco's history as the man who first introduced plays, operas and great theater to the West. **TS**

OSTRICH FEVER

Billie Frantz was a successful chicken rancher working near Anaheim, California, in 1882. One day his wife decided to go shopping — and what she brought back changed Billie's life.

Imagine how, when she returned to the ranch after her spree in town, Mrs. Frantz might have said, "Look at this, Billie! I'm going to have the milliner put it on my new hat!"

Billie would have looked and scratched his head. "Now what kind of a chicken would grow a thing like that?"

"It's an ostrich feather, silly! It cost $15."

"$15? Why, I wouldn't pay that for ..."

Billie did some arithmetic. If one feather cost $15, and a bird had 30 or 40 feathers – well,

Ostrich Farm

it was a lot of money. So Billie set to work and imported 22 ostriches from South Africa.

But raising ostriches was a whole lot different than raising chickens. Billie had to put up nine-foot-tall redwood fences since the strange-looking creatures could — and often did — kick down any ordinary fence and easily hurt themselves in the process. If they got out, Billie discovered, you had to catch them, and they could outrun the fastest horses. Even worse, Billie had to sell his prize fox-hounds because the dogs made the ostriches nervous.

But Billie managed, and not only did he make a bundle of profit on ostrich feathers, he also hatched 16 chicks from his first ostriches. Soon his rancher friends began to buy the chicks. Before long, 6,000 ostriches lived on ranches all over southern California.

That was a lot of feathers — and, wouldn't you know it, just about then Mrs. Frantz began adorning her hats with something else. Ostrich feathers were going out of style. But oranges were becoming popular to eat, so the ranchers turned to raising the profitable fruits instead. Today, you can still see what remains of the orange orchards — but except for a few in the zoos, there aren't many ostriches. **TS**

WYOMING WOMEN

You've got to hand it to the people of Wyoming territory in the 1800s — they decided early on that women should have the right to vote, which is called "suffrage." Then they defended their policy against a shocked federal government.

In the middle years of that century, half a million or more folks traveled through Wyoming. Usually they were on their way to somewhere else — California or Texas or maybe Oregon. But some of them looked around and decided to settle down in the vast, open plains. The area was granted territorial status in 1868.

The area was quite progressive for its time. The men decided that their wives, mothers and sisters were just as hardworking and valuable as they were, and they began wondering why the women weren't allowed to vote. They were nudged along by Esther Hobart Morris, who invited the territory's legislators to a tea party and convinced them that granting their women suffrage would increase the voting power of law-abiding citizens. In the wild and lawless West, Wyoming politicians found it was a good argument.

A few years later, Wyoming Territory was prospering, and its residents decided it had outgrown mere territorial status. They wanted to become a full state, the 44th state in the Union. Congress was fully behind the idea until it realized Wyoming was a place where women were allowed to vote! During the debates, one congressmember rose and asked, "Can a place that allows its *women* the unrestricted right to *vote*, and to hold *public office* and sit on *juries* — can such a state be trusted with full partnership in the Union?"

Wyoming answered, in effect, "It sure can!" Congress frowned and told Wyoming that it could come in as a state only if it got rid of woman suffrage. But Wyoming didn't hesitate;

they told the federal government that they would come in with their women voters or not at all. It took the feds until 1890 to give in, and then the state of Wyoming took its rightful place in the Union.

In 1925, the people of Wyoming took another giant leap in the history of women's equality and elected the nation's first woman governor, Nellie Tayloe Ross. Wyoming is very proud of its heritage: The state motto is "Equal Rights," and its nickname is "The Equality State."

As for Esther Morris, who started it all — suffrage was just the beginning. In 1870, Morris became the first woman justice of the peace in world history. There is a statue of her in front of the capitol at Cheyenne, Wyoming. **TS**

Early Leaders Of The Woman's Suffrage Movement

THE REPUBLICAN ORATOR
MEETS HIS MATCH

Theodore Roosevelt

Political put-downs, even the clever ones, can sometimes backfire. One of our presidents found that out when he let loose a remark that returned to bite him.

Teddy Roosevelt, our first President Roosevelt, visited the Northwest in May of 1903. The famed old Denny Hotel had just been modernized and renamed "The Washington." Teddy was one of its first guests — and he was impressed.

He said to one of his aides, "Why, this is bully! This Seattle is a thriving little city!"

The aide replied, "It is, Mr. President. It's been growing fast and is going to keep on growing. And they've got a smart engineer who's built the water and sewer systems far larger than they need now to meet the needs of the future."

Teddy flashed his famous glittery-teeth smile and turned to editing his speech for that night. It would boost his Republican Party.

As expected, the crowd was big and enthusiastic. Teddy was an exciting and popular figure in

America. The speech started well. There was applause, hand-waving and banners. On the fringe of the crowd, though, was a shabby-looking man who kept heckling the president. He yelled, "I'm a Socialist!"

The president finally smiled at the man and asked politely, "May I ask the gentleman why he is a Socialist?"

The heckler called back, "Certainly, certainly. My granpappy was a Socialist, and my pappy was a Socialist, and I'm a Socialist!"

Once more, the famous smile spread across Roosevelt's face. "I see. And if your granpappy had been a jackass, and your pappy a jackass, what would you be?"

The heckler quickly replied, "I'd be a Republican!" It took five minutes for the laughter to quiet. The famous put-down went around the world. Teddy won the election, anyway. But the quick-witted — if boisterous — citizen shuffled off, and was never heard from again. **TS**

THE ANDERSON AND HER CAPTAIN

In the Midwest, everyone knows of the famous paddle-wheeler the *Robert E. Lee*. In the Northwest, it's the *Eliza Anderson* that has the claim to fame, and rightly so.

Puget Sound's "mosquito fleet" started up around 1853. The fleet of tiny steamers moved freight and passengers between Olympia and Seattle and waypoints in-between. Many of the small ships blew up or ran ashore on the rocks, but not the sturdy *Anderson*, which ran as far as Victoria, B.C.. Folks said she moved slower — and made money faster — than any other vessel in the history of the Sound.

The *Anderson* was quite a character. Her salty Captain Finch installed a steam calliope on her deck, and she carried a musician who would tootle popular tunes of the time. You could hear the *Anderson* coming an hour before her arrival;

people preparing for a journey on the boat liked that because it forewarned them when to get their luggage and freight down to the wharf. The Native Americans of the areas were fascinated by it as well; they would paddle down in their canoes to listen.

Captain Finch was big on other public services, especially when he benefited as well. For example, the University of Washington was just getting off to a rocky start in 1860. There was little money and few students to go around. Captain Finch made a deal with the university, which had acres and acres of trees on its land. He would buy the wood for his ship's boilers at a low price and the university would keep a portion of the money, paying the rest out to hired students. It was a good deal for all involved.

One legendary act of the good captain came about on a terribly stormy night when Finch was bucking the *Anderson,* heavily loaded with passengers and freight, through Deception Pass. The freight included eight head of cattle, seven pianos and 12 barrels of whiskey. The ship was in trouble, taking water and about to founder. The passengers clung white-faced to their seats as the ship rocked to and fro. From the pilot house, the captain shouted, "Overboard with the cattle!" The cattle were pushed overboard. A bit later, he shouted again, "Overboard with the pianos!" Over went the pianos. The lightened ship got safely to port.

Later, the insurance investigator asked him, "Captain Finch, don't you think you should have thrown the whiskey barrels overboard and saved the pianos?"

The captain glared at him as if he were ignorant. "You can't drink *pianos!*" **TS**

SKAE'S SECRET

Suppose you found out that two multimillionaires were talking secretly about a fabulous deal that no one else knew of. And suppose that deal could mean a fortune to you. A man named John Skae was in that position — and he became rich.

There was a good deal of gold and silver money around in the 1870s, and a good chunk of it was held by Jim Fair and John Mackay. These two men lived in Virginia City, and they often pulled strings and wires to get control of profitable mining operations. They had two San Francisco partners with whom they kept in touch by telegraph. To make sure no one could read their messages, they sent them in a secret code. Anyone who happened to look at their messages would have seen only a jumble of letters. You'd have to decipher it to learn that Fair and Mackay had just acquired the rights to an enormously rich silver mine.

Well, John Skae did just that. He was an obscure telegraph clerk who may have learned something about code-breaking in the army during the Civil War. It's also possible that he figured it out on his own. At any rate, Skae decoded a telegram about Fair and Mackay's mining bonanza.

Skae scraped together all the cash he had and borrowed more. He bought all the stock in the mine that he could. In no time at all, news of the mine's wealth went out, and the stock began its astonishing climb. Two hundred, five, nine . . . a thousand dollars a share! Skae went to a broker, sold his stock and walked out with $3 million .

Skae began living it up in a big way. He did some speculating, too. Now all he could pick, though, were losers. He was almost broke when he heard of another great bonanza stock. He told his broker to buy it; it was 50¢ a share. Not too long afterward, it hit $273 a share! His broker recommended that he sell, pointing out that he was worth over $1 million. Skae refused, believing the stock would go higher. He held and held as the stock climbed and climbed. Then suddenly the stock nose-dived, and Skae lost everything.

He never got to try a third time at making a million. From that day on, Skae never bought another share of stock in any company. **TS**

FENCED OUT

Nicholas Yung was a home-loving undertaker. No one would have remembered him if he hadn't inspired a strange San Francisco city ordinance — one that is still on the books.

By the mid-1860s, the huge gold rush in the California mountains had faded in the light of new discoveries in Gold Hill, Colorado; Virginia City, Nevada; Orofino, Idaho; and Virginia City, Montana. Much of the Mother Lode gold was gone from San Francisco and now in vaults in the East, but at the same time the "little city by the bay" had grown into a metropolis. It was filled with businesses, banks, shipping centers, construction companies and industry of all kinds. San Francisco was the hub of the West, and Nob Hill was where the city's new millionaires wanted to build their mansions.

Wealthy Charles Crocker owned an entire block on Nob Hill at California and Mason

Streets, having bought it piece by piece — all except for the one narrow lot belonging to Nicholas Yung. Crocker was planning to join the other millionaires there on Nob Hill with the magnificent home he had planned. He told Yung he wanted to buy his house and the lot on which it sat.

The negotiation might have gone something

The Crocker Mansion

like this: "Mr. Yung, my appraiser has looked at your property, and he says $3,000 is a fair price. Will you sell it to me for $3,000?"

Yung shook his head. "I like my property, and I don't want to sell it. If you said $6,000,

though, I might think about it."

Crocker said, "All right, $6,000. Think about it."

A few days later, Yung came to Crocker and said, "I think maybe that's not enough either. Make it $9,000, and I'll think some more."

Crocker grumbled, but he agreed. When the price got to $25,000, and Yung was still thinking, Crocker snarled, "Forget it!" and built his great mansion anyway. But he also built a 40-foot-high fence on his own property, surrounding three sides of Yung's lot. This shut off all Yung's sunlight and a good deal of his fresh air.

Yung and his attorneys realized that he didn't have a good legal case, and that even if he did Crocker could tie him up in court for years. Yung grumbled behind his 40-foot-high enclosure for a long time. Then he finally sold his piece of land to Crocker at a reasonable price and bought some property further away.

The story didn't end there, though. Freedom-loving San Franciscans thought Crocker had played a dirty game. They got the city supervisors to pass the famous Spite Fence Law that to this day prohibits anyone in the city from building a fence above a reasonable height without special permission.

No one today knows for sure exactly where Yung's old house stood. And Crocker's magnificent mansion? The site is now occupied by the beautiful Grace Cathedral. **TS**

GLAMOROUS HOLLYWOOD

The name of the town conjures thoughts of fabulously beautiful stars, exotic homes, public adoration — exciting, daring, imaginative Hollywood! But it wasn't always so; in fact, for a while it was quite the reverse.

It was the climate that brought early moviemakers like D. W. Griffith to southern California in the 1910s and early '20s. While the East Coast suffered long winter storms, southern California provided good light and nice weather that made for easier filming. In the first three months of 1910, 21 movies were made in California's mountains, orange groves, missions and along its seashores.

The influx of these film pioneers was not at all appreciated by the local residents. One local reporter called the film-makers "an impudent, troublesome, harum-scarum lot, and an unmitigated nuisance!"

Actually, that reporter wasn't far wrong. Movie companies did shoot scenes wherever and whenever they pleased. Their camera crews and their bulky light reflectors snarled traffic. Another reporter buttonholed the director of such a crew that was creating a traffic jam. "Tell me," the reporter asked, "what's the story you're making here?"

The director replied, "No special story. We shoot scenes we like, and make it up as we go along."

In fact, in those days, no responsible father would allow his daughter to go out with a man in the movie industry — or even allow such a man in his house. Signs on rooming houses read, "No dogs or actors allowed."

Early Picture Studio In California

So it's not surprising that it was hard for movie-makers to find places to set up studios, since most areas of Los Angeles didn't want them around. Several companies tried to set up studios in an obscure little neighborhood with only 4,000 residents — a place called Hollywood. Although the local people objected strenuously, a few companies did manage to put down roots there.

The big change came when Griffith made the great classic silent film *Birth of a Nation* in 1915. The landmark film heralded the beginning of the new art form of cinema. The huge international success of his film broke down suburban resistance. Suddenly producers needed more scripts, directors needed more staff and people were needed to build sets, to apply makeup and even to make coffee. There were plentiful jobs for writers, actors, camera operators, carpenters and many other craftspeople.

Sleepy little Hollywood grew bigger by the thousands. By the mid-1920s, Hollywood films had bigger profits than the local orange groves. Many fine actors, seasoned by the theater on Broadway, came west. Charlie Chaplin, Douglas Fairbanks, Jesse Lasky, Theda Bara and Rudolph Valentino became household names. Among Griffith's troupe of fine actors was the silent film star Mary Pickford. Cecil B. DeMille's stars included Gloria Swanson and Ramon Navarro. And around that time Walt Disney was working on animations of a certain mouse that would some day be famous. Hollywood became known around the world: It was definitely glamorous and now (almost) respectable. **TS**

STRANGE LIGHT

The tower must have looked like something left here by alien beings.

San Jose, California, was a small agricultural town back in 1881. But it was right up-to-date, with its horse cars and gas-lighted parlors. What's more, it had a far-seeing, conscientious board of supervisors and mayor. Like most leaders of the Old West, they had a strong sense of civic pride and were not afraid to try something new.

On May 13, 1881, J. J. Owen, the editor of the *San Jose Mercury* newspaper, printed an editorial stating that the city would be improved if it was better lit at night: Crime would virtually disappear if the back streets, vacant lots and alleys were exposed, preventing criminals from lurking there. He suggested that a large tower should be built, with lamps at the top that would throw a radiance rival to the sun. The supervisors and mayor quickly agreed and construction on the project began.

The 237-foot San Jose Electric Light Tower was completed and lit on December 13, 1881. With an intensity of 24,000 candlepower, the tower illuminated the area — it stood at the intersection of Santa Clara and Market Streets — but didn't really light the whole town. Nevertheless it was a success, and people came from all over to look at this symbol of progress, this new source of power. It's even been said that Gustave Eiffel, the builder of the famous tower in Paris, came to see the San Jose tower for ideas.

Just about now, a fellow named Thomas Edison was hard at work inventing the electric light bulb. A more practical source of illumination, the light bulb would soon be used by cities in streetlights. But the magnificent and strange tower stood in San Jose as a landmark until 1915, when, weakened by a storm, it collapsed into the street. **TS**

San Jose Electric Light Tower

THE GREAT LUGGAGE CASE

Ever traveled to Chicago — and found out your baggage went to Albuquerque? Losing baggage is nothing new. In fact, in 1850, one of the first cases decided by the California Supreme Court tackled this very problem.

Benjamin Farley was a bank clerk in upstate New York. He wanted very much to marry his sweetheart, but his income was hardly enough to keep him in top hats. He decided to make his fortune in the California gold rush, but not as a miner. He figured that with thousands of men rushing into the state, there'd be a lot of building going on. Farley decided to use the $400 he had saved to buy nails in New York and then go sell them in California for a huge profit. He was sure he'd be back within a year, and his darling promised to wait for him forever. He bought the nails and left with them on a Pacific Mail Company steamship.

The voyage was brutal. The storms ripped through sails; the ship's boilers balked. Farley was violently ill, and the food served on the ship made him even more ill. When he finally reached San Francisco, pale, weak and 15 pounds lighter, he went to claim his nails, which had been stashed in the hold. The shipping clerk just looked at him blankly and said, "What nails?"

Farley sued the shipping line, asking for $1,200 for the value of the lost nails plus the line's failure to provide the "first-class cuisine" promised in their advertising. The jury awarded $1,000 to Farley. The judge, however, thought that was too much and changed the award to $400.

Farley appealed to the just-established California Supreme Court. There, Justice Hastings ruled that lower-court justices should only change award amounts when they are obviously unjust or based on fraud — not the case with Farley's nails. And so Farley got his $1,000.

He didn't, however, get his sweetheart. "Forever" to her meant only until she met and married a wealthy stockbroker. Farley invested his $1,000 in land in the sparsely-settled western part of San Francisco and became rich, although he remained a bachelor for the rest of his long life. **TS**

COMMODORE JONES'S WAR

The most embarrassed hero in all United States Naval history has got to be Commodore Thomas Catesby Jones. It wasn't all his fault, though. Today we would say he was "done in by a communication glitch."

You see, back in 1842, Mexico had owed the United States money for some time — but it couldn't pay. At the same time, Washington, D. C., lawmakers worried that the Mexican government would hand California over to the British for safekeeping. There was talk of war between the U. S. and Mexico.

The news reached Commodore Jones in Peru when he got a dispatch on the subject. The way *he* read the dispatch, war had been declared. Never one to hang back, the commodore rushed his warships along the coast to Monterey. If anyone could save California from the English, he was the one.

On October 19, 1842, Jones reached Monterey, which was then the capital of California. He marched into the town without a shot being fired. The Mexican town mayor, known in Spanish as the *alcalde* (all-call-day), greeted him and no doubt invited him to have a glass of wine. The commodore frowned and declared something to the effect of, "Sir, there is a state of war. I am capturing this city."

"A war, Commodore?" The *alcalde* was astonished. "I haven't heard. Well, make yourself at home anyway, while I check into this. Of course, you and your officers are invited to stay for dinner!"

Next morning, the conquering hero learned the truth. There was no war. It had all been a mistake. He apologized profusely and sailed to San Pedro, where he paid a humble visit to the Mexican official overseeing the region, Governor Micheltorena. Jones and his officers enjoyed an amiable visit with the governor and his family. The event was forgiven and forgotten, except by the brave commodore, whose face must have been red for a long, long time. **TS**

CHEYENNE FASHIONS

The first white men who traveled and explored the West were tough, practical, no-nonsense men who were not interested in trivialities. Lewis Gerrard, who wandered the Santa Fe trail in the 1840s, had these qualities, too, but sometimes he found himself drawn to the lighter side of life. When Gerrard encountered the Cheyenne Indians of the western mountains, he wrote an accurate record of everything he saw — including notes on local fashions!

Gerrard visited the Cheyenne villages and found the people to be hospitable and friendly. They were especially friendly if you brought coffee with you — which Gerrard always did.

Gerrard recounted how the village periodically moved to another location. Each lodge had its own band of horses, some pulling *travees* (sleds) loaded with baggage and laughing *papooses* (babies). He wrote, "The young squaws take

**Cheyenne Indians
Dressed For Ceremonial Dance**

much care of their dress and horse equipment. They dash furiously past on wild steeds ... and the riders show admirable daring."

"Their dresses were buckskin, high at the neck, [with] short sleeves or no sleeves at all, fitting loosely to the knee, the edges scalloped, worked with beads and fringed," he went on. "They wore tightly fitted leggings and neat moccasins, handsomely worked with beads. They wore glittering brass bracelets and Pacific shells in their pierced ears." He even remarked upon the dramatic appearance of the women's hair: "Their fine complections [sic] were eclipsed by a coat of flaming vermillion [red]."

Gerrard wrote that it was, overall, "A pleasing and desirable change from the sight of the pinched waists and constrained motions of the women of the States, to see these daughters of the prairie dressed loosely, free to act, unconfined by the ligatures of fashion."

"Of course," he hastened to add, "it's not that I would like to see *our* women dressed *à la Cheyenne*, but where novelty constitutes the charm, 'twas indeed a relief to the eye." Thus ended the fashion report from New Mexico in the 1840s. **TS**

MR. WO GOES TO WASHINGTON

He was probably just another immigrant arriving in San Francisco by ship from Canton, China. And, as many others did, he opened a steam laundry. But this immigrant went from starching shirts in his place of business to arguing justice before the United States Supreme Court, and he made legal history. His name was Yick Wo.

In those days of fast growth and wooden buildings, there were a lot of fires in San Francisco. There was also a lot of laundry — along with boiler explosions in the laundry facilities. So in 1880, San Francisco passed a law requiring that all the steam laundries be licensed for safety. However, there was one problem with how the law was carried out. All of the laundries were being operated safely — but only about half of the operators were given licenses. Mr. Yick Wo was in the other half, and without one of those licenses he couldn't operate his business and therefore couldn't feed his family. He decided to sue.

His lawyer asked the city clerk some pointed questions. He found out that the clerk had granted 170 licenses, none of which were to non-citizen Chinese laundry operations. The clerk had denied 150 licenses, all to non-citizen Chinese operations. It was clear that no non-citizen Chinese was granted a license and that no applicant of European descent was denied one. When the lawyer asked why this had been the case, the clerk told him it was the policy of the Board of Supervisors. But the lawyer knew better. It was simply racism.

In the first trial, the court decided against Yick Wo, but his lawyer appealed, and the case went all the way to the United States Supreme Court. The high court came down hard on the San Francisco supervisors. It said, "It's proper and legal to regulate boiler operations — that's a matter of public safety. But it is *not* proper and legal to discriminate unjustly. That is very clear here. The lower court is reversed. The clerk is ordered to issue licenses to all who operate boilers safely, regardless of race."

That was over a century ago, but Yick Wo has not been forgotten. His name has been given to a San Francisco school, a fitting memorial for the city that learned a valuable lesson about justice. **TS**

LETHAL LASSOES

You've seen them in movies and at rodeos — cowboys with lassoes, roping and tying steers in a matter of seconds. Some people, however, have seen the lasso used as a weapon of war.

In the early 1800s, the lasso, called a *reata* in Spanish, was used by the cowboys or *gauchos* throughout the Spanish colonies in the Americas. The *reata* was woven together of thin leather strips and was about as thick as your little finger. You'd tie one end to your saddle horn and keep a running knot at the other. If you were out for a steer or a bear, you'd hold the *reata* coiled in one hand and gallop at your quarry while twirling the other end over your head. You'd let the rope fly, catch your target and drag it along with you.

Strangely enough, this simple contraption put down an impromptu invasion of Buenos Aires, Argentina, by the British. In June 1806,

Sir Home Popham was leading his men back to the British Isles from a military expedition in Cape Town, South Africa, when he decided to make an attack on Buenos Aires. At that time, Argentina was owned by Spain, which was at war with Britain. Popham saw an opportunity to take the city and, in effect, the entire country from the Spanish. Without waiting for orders from London, he attacked. When news of his action reached London, the British leaders imme-diately sent reinforcements to Popham's aide.

Cowboy With Herd

However, after two months of quiet planning, the city residents suddenly launched a full resistance to the British Invasion. They quickly surrounded British General George Beresford and his forces on land, while Popham watched from his ship, which was anchored in the estuary beside the city. The Argentineans soon formed an ad hoc militia of 8,000 civilians under the leadership of Santiago Liniers, a French-born soldier in the Spanish army. Using their lassoes, among other weapons, the Argentineans kept the British forces down.

The furious British commander, berating his men when they balked at his com-mand, probably said something like, "I want you men to get ready to attack! What's the matter with you? These are not soldiers you're fighting, they don't know warfare — they're just shop-keepers and cowboys, for heaven's sake!"

A sergeant might have spoken up. "Sir, it isn't the bullets we're scared of. These *gauchos*, they're impossible to fight! They lurk out of gun-shot range, and when you've shot your shot and you're ramming in more powder and ball, they come at you with their darned ropes! You're just lifting your musket and whoosh — a *gaucho's* got you dragging at full speed over the rocks, scream-ing something dreadful. It's a terrible way for a soldier to die, sir."

The British reinforcements, under the com-mand of General George Whitelocke, didn't fare any better. They were quickly shot down with arms that the Argentineans had captured from the earlier invaders. It wasn't long before the British decided they had more important busi-ness elsewhere — thanks in part to the rope-twirling abilities of the defenders of Buenos Aires. **TS**

WILD BILL AND THE DEADLY POKER HAND

His actual name was James Butler Hickok, but they called him "Wild Bill" instead. This notorious lawman of the Old West had a penchant for getting into trouble — and that's exactly what happened when he sat down to a certain game of poker one day.

Wild Bill Hickok grew up in Illinois. As a boy, he helped his father with transporting run-away slaves on the underground railroad. In 1855, he continued this cause, joining the Redlegs, an anti-slavery gang in Kansas. Wild Bill eventually became one of the West's typical U.S. marshals. As they all had to be, he was tough, afraid of nothing and he carried a fast gun. He'd been a Union scout during the Civil War and afterward he moved west with the frontier.

Wild Bill Hickok

It was 1876, in Deadwood, South Dakota, that Wild Bill played a friendly hand of poker that cost him more than his winnings. Concentrating on the game, Wild Bill sat in Saloon No. 10, facing away from the door. As he focused intently at the cards in his hand, he didn't notice a man enter the saloon. Before anyone knew what had happened, the man shot Wild Bill from behind, killing him.

The shooter was Jack McCall, a poor loser who had gambled away $110 to Wild Bill the day before. After the ruthless shooting, McCall was promptly tried and sentenced to be hanged. His appeal bought him a year of life, but after a second trial he was executed.

The card game will never be forgotten, however. The cards that Wild Bill were holding at the time of his murder were all black aces and eights — a hand that's known today as the "dead man's hand." **TS**

BLACK JACK PERSHING

The men of Troop H, 10th Cavalry, wondered one day in 1886 about their new officer. These cavalrymen were tough and experienced, and they wanted a leader who was also tough and knew his business. There was no other way for a leader to be in the great Southwest.

The troop was made up of African-American soldiers, and they were hoping that they would finally get a few African-American officers. When Lieutenant Black Jack Pershing arrived next morning, they were disappointed. But as it turned out, he and the soldiers of Troop H got along just fine.

They carried out the near-impossible job of finding fugitive bands of Native Americans holding out against forced relocation to Canada. Pershing and his soldiers searched for Apache and Sioux under a blazing prairie sun. Patiently keeping their tempers in check, they persuaded the bands to surrender, all without a single shot being fired. Years later, Pershing — by then a general — wrote that his association with the officers and men of the 10th Cavalry was of greatest value to him.

In the meantime, however, Pershing had led his men up San Juan Hill in Cuba in 1898, vitally assisting Teddy Roosevelt and his Rough Riders during the Spanish-American War. They also chased bandits across the Mexican border in 1917 with limited success.

Within the next decade, America was on the verge of World War I, and when war came, Black Jack Pershing was the general of the armies, of vital help in turning back a furious German offensive.

Black Jack Pershing

As chief of staff, Pershing was honored throughout America and the world. He even won a Pulitzer Prize in history for his book, *My Experiences in the World War*. But he never forgot his service with the African-American regiment. He took great pride in its fine performance over the years and helped win commissions for 62 non-commissioned officers of the 10th Cavalry, 20 of them as captains. **TS**

LEGENDARY PANTS

Everyone knows that a lot of money was made on gold in California in the mid-1800s, but one famous fellow found his fortune there in a rather unlikely way. He struck it big manufacturing a new kind of clothing — denim jeans.

When news of the gold rush reached New York in 1849, the three Strauss brothers decided that one of them should go west as well. They weren't going for the gold; instead, they planned to sell dry goods. Perhaps the brothers figured the gold seekers would be especially short on shelter; they might strike it rich selling tents. The plan was set that one brother, Levi, would voyage around the horn of South America up to San Francisco carrying among his cargo heavy canvas cloth. The story goes that once Levi reached San Francisco and his business took off, he would send back to his brothers for more material for the tents.

Popular myth has it that once Levi reached San Francisco he discovered that, because of the mild climate, the miners and other workers didn't really need tents. What was he to do with his cargo of canvas? For some time, legend recorded that Levi found the answer when a prospector told him about one item that was sorely needed in the mining fields — pants! People needed pants that would hold up in the mines, where the thinner cotton and wool trousers didn't last. Levi's tough, sturdy canvas would make ideal work pants. At this point, some people have claimed that Levi rushed to a tailor and had several dozen pairs of canvas pants made up. As the prospectors found out about the pants, Levi's new merchandise quickly sold out. Levi thought he had hit it big. The story goes that Levi then changed to a more suitable kind of cloth called *serge de Nimes*, which soon became known as "denim," and the pants sold even better. But things weren't quite ready for success — complaints soon started coming back.

The pockets kept pulling out of the pants — quite a problem, since miners and other working men carried all sorts of heavy, essential items in their pockets.

Historical sources dispute how Levi actually started his career in manufacturing jeans, and the idea that he used canvas from his dry goods business is likely nothing more than myth. It is clear, however, that at some point he was consulted by an expert tailor from Nevada, a man named Jacob Davis. Davis had been selling pants to miners in Nevada and had come up with an idea for how to make the clothing stronger: He wanted to use copper rivets to strengthen the fabric at seams that were especially stressed. Davis hoped to patent his idea, but he didn't have enough money to file for the patent. Somehow he connected with Levi, who believed the rivets would solve the problems he'd been having with his own pants. Levi readily agreed to join him as a business partner. Soon almost every man in the state of California was wearing the denim pants with the riveted pockets.

Levi's ingenuity led to the rise of a world-recognized industry. A century-and-a-half later, you can still buy a pair of Levi's jeans. And even though the modern essentials you carry in your pockets today don't really require them anymore, those rivets are still used as a classic feature that defines jeans. **TS**

SHANGHAI KELLY

The trouble with the Great Gold Rush of the 1850s was that everyone came to California and no one wanted to leave. For example, the men who sailed the ships around South America and into San Francisco Bay harbor were harder to keep hold of than slippery fish — a captain would sail his boat in and, as soon as the anchor dropped in the harbor, his crew was off to the mines never to return.

In fact, there were 600 ships abandoned in the Bay in 1850. How did the deserted sea captains manage to sail those ships out of San Francisco without their crews? Well, some captains dropped by to see Shanghai Kelly. This character ran a highly profitable boarding house and saloon overlooking the bay, but he made the bulk of his loot by supplying sailors for a price.

His method was simple: He'd see a likely looking lad in his saloon, then he'd give him a drink that was altered with sleeping powder. Minutes later, Kelly would drop the unconscious seaman-to-be through a trapdoor out into a boat that was waiting in the water below the saloon. In the morning, the lad would awaken far out on the Pacific.

Kelly's biggest coup came when he got orders for crews for three ships at once — a difficult assignment when all the men in sight were headed for the gold fields. So one evening Kelly invited the entire crowd in the bar to a special event. To celebrate his birthday, he announced to everyone, he was going to have a big party aboard the paddlewheeler *Goliath*. Everyone was invited. There would be barrels of whiskey, all the food you could eat, music, everything!

It was a lure that no one could refuse. The next day, once 90 men had come aboard the *Goliath* and sampled the drinks, Kelly simply gave the order to haul up the anchor and cast off. It was a great but very short-lived party. After the sleep-inducing drinks took effect, Kelley

Pier At San Francisco Waterfront

delivered his unconscious cargo to each of the three ships. He collected his fees (about $30,000, tax-free) and returned to port and his thriving business in rooms, liquor and sailors.

Shanghai Kelley may have made a lot of money through these nefarious means, but it's a fair guess that nobody *ever* attended his birthday parties after that! **TS**

OWNING ARIZONA

One lovely spring day in the early 1880s, the citizens of Phoenix, Arizona, got a terrible shock. A distinguished gentleman named James Reavis just up and announced publicly, "I am the legal owner of this entire city. I have all the papers to prove it!"

Legal notices were printed in the newspaper and placed all over town. At first, people thought it was a big joke and laughed at the idea. But Reavis *did* have papers, records, deeds and grants going back many years to King Philip IV of Spain. The ancient papers showed that the king had handed out vast lands in America to his friends, among them the head of a Spanish noble family named Don Miguel de Peralta. Through his dealings in land, Reavis had acquired these deeds. Reassuring the city that he would be a reasonable man, Reavis said something like, "You can keep your houses, land and buildings if you pay me for a legal release."

Reasonable or not, some of the city's prominent citizens wanted more proof before handing over huge amounts of cash. They met with Joseph Robbins, the surveyor general for land-grant claims, and asked him to examine Reavis's trunkful of papers. Based on what the surveyor general studied over the next few days, he had to conclude, "Gentlemen, I am not an expert. But my staff and I have examined these documents very carefully. We found that the earliest documents are written unquestion- ably in the Spanish of 200 years ago, not in mod- ern Spanish. They were definitely written in the proper ink, and the paper is without question the paper of the peri- od. What is also against us is the fact that many of the supporting documents are duplicated in the official public records kept since the days of Miguel de Peralta."

The citizens and their lawyers looked at each other. Finally one said, "Gentlemen, I think we'd be smart to settle now, before this man's prices go up." Some did settle. For example, Southern Pacific paid Reavis $50,000. Still

Birds Eye View Of Arizona

others were made of sterner stuff. They hired document experts and detectives.

They found that Reavis had slipped up and had — as often happens in mystery stories — made one little mistake. Supposedly written in the 1600s, certain key names and statements on Reavis's documents had been written with a steel pen — an invention that didn't exist until 1800.

The whole fraud unraveled. Reavis had spent years preparing his scheme. He had studied archaic Spanish, mastered the old style of writing and had gotten a job with a government bureau where he could doctor original documents. It was a brilliant performance, but in the end the sheriff came to get him with a warrant for his arrest on the grounds of criminal fraud. Instead of Reavis collecting money for Phoenix, Phoenix collected Reavis — and dumped him in prison for six years. **TS**

TALKING MIRRORS

Years ago, newswriters who couldn't think of anything else to write about made up science fiction stories about "death rays"– lethal beams that would wipe out armies and win wars. Actually these newswriters were closer to truth than they ever realized: The U.S. Army had a non-lethal ray machine way back in the 1880s — and it *did* help win a war.

In those days, the Apache Indians, led by the great Geronimo, raided many southwestern Arizona settlements and killed the settlers. Geronimo was a shrewd, courageous war leader who used strategy and his tough warriors as well as any four-star general. One thing, though, put fear into his heart, and that was evil spirits. He had seen flashes of light on the mountaintops in broad daylight, and he believed they were spirits that must be carefully avoided.

The day came when General Nelson Miles

and Geronimo met under a flag of truce. Miles told the chief of the many technological advancements of the U.S. Army in an attempt to persuade him to agree to a peace treaty. Miles spoke of the steam-engine trains that let the army move troops very quickly across the country. He talked of the telegraph as a means of instantaneous communication. But most significantly, he told Geronimo about a device called the heliostat. The heliostat was a mirror with a shutter arrangement; the operator could reflect the sun's rays in the mirror and click the shutter slowly or quickly to form dots and dashes for sending Morse code messages, like a telegraph machine. Miles' heliostat system could send 25-word messages 400 miles over a zigzag course and could receive an answer within four hours.

Miles demonstrated the system for Geronimo by sending a message and receiving a reply. He told Geronimo how his scouts could watch the Indians' movements and quickly relay messages about them over the tops of the moun-

Geronimo

tains, across a distance that would take a man on a swift pony 20 days to travel. Geronimo kept a passive face, but he must have been stunned by the demonstration of what he had for so long believed to be the work of spirits. It's possible that he decided it was useless to struggle against a country that could command such powers.

General Miles's report said that after seeing this demonstration, Geronimo sent a message to his brother Natchez, who was hidden in the mountains. A few hours later, Natchez came into camp with the Apache warriors and families, and a final treaty of peace was worked out.

The military still uses a similar instrument. Called a heliograph, it has a powerful searchlight behind the shutter so it can be used at night. **TS**

ALL THE PRESIDENT'S FRIENDS

It has been said there are three essential elements to life as we know it: air, water and oil. In the early part of this century, southern California was wallowing in oil — and the crooks were wallowing in money.

President Harding had nice-enough manners, and he certainly looked the part of president. Unfortunately, he appointed to high offices some men who cheated at everything.

When he went from Ohio to Washington, D.C., in 1921, Harding, innocently enough, brought in a high-level crew of officials later known as the Ohio Gang. Here the scene shifts to Elk Hills, and Buena Vista, (near Bakersfield) California, and to Teapot Dome in Wyoming. These were government oil reserve areas to be used by the Navy in time of war.

Harding appointed a man named Albert B. Fall to one of his Cabinet posts. Fall made a secret deal with his friend Edward Doheny, president of Pan-American Petroleum. Fall leased him two of the government's oil fields. The third oil field was leased to Harry Sinclair of Mammoth Oil. Overall, the deal was worth at least $120 million at the time. Before long, Fall had bought a racehorse and was living such a lavish lifestyle that his next-door neighbors couldn't help noticing.

Other members of the "gang" pursued other secret deals involving the Veterans Bureau and the Office of the Alien Property Custodian. Luckily, there were also clever, honest politicians around. Senator Thomas Walsh and Senator Burton Wheeler, for example, were skillful detective-prosecutors, and they peeled the conspiracies down layer by layer. The crooks threw up many obstacles: They bribed at least

President Warren Harding And His Cabinet

one juror, tapped telephones and faked evidence. It took years for government prosecutors to bring Fall and Sinclair to trial. Fall was fined and sentenced to one year in jail, but Sinclair and Doheny were acquitted. Meanwhile, an old friend of Harding, Attorney General Harry Daugherty, resigned from his post when charges of corruption came against him; he was later implicated in illegal activities involving the acquisition of money through unfair means.

Did President Harding know of his friends' corruption? Probably not for quite a while. But in the last few weeks of his life, he looked worried and depressed. He asked what a president should do when his friends betray him. Harding was touring the country when he died quite suddenly in San Francisco at his suite in the Palace Hotel. The official version is that he died of a heart attack — but many people, then and now, think it might have been heartbreak instead. **TS**

THE FORGOTTEN EXPLORER

Had Spanish Admiral Alejandro Malaspina been like other explorers, he probably would have died young but left behind a legacy of adventure tales. Instead, poor Malaspina lived long but never got the credit for his remarkable voyage to America's Pacific Northwest in the late 1700s.

Malaspina was not just an unusually able sea captain; he also enjoyed working with scientists and physicians. He obtained better instruments for navigation and better diets for his crew. For his five-year voyage to America, he recruited a team of outstanding mapmakers, artists, naturalists, astronomers and others.

Also, unlike most early explorers, Malaspina was not after gold or slaves. What he brought back to Spain was a different kind of treasure — reams of information about the lands he'd seen. His maps of the coast were marvels of accuracy for the time. They compare remarkably well with aerial photos of the area made today!

The good admiral received a royal welcome on his return to Spain. King Carlos IV praised him and invited him to visit court. Malaspina was a great favorite at first, but then the whispers began. The other courtiers didn't agree with Malaspina's support of freedom for the Spanish colonies. Even more scandalous was the fact that he was overshadowing another courtier, Señor Godoy, as the queen's favorite. The jealous Godoy showed King Carlos an intimate note that he said Malaspina had written to the queen. The king had Malaspina arrested at once.

Malaspina managed to save his neck, but he lost all his honors and his rank. He was exiled from Spain and spent his last 15 years in the Italian village of Pontremoli, where he had been born. When his valuable and scholarly report of the Pacific Northwest was finally published, the name of Malaspina was nowhere to be seen on it.

But Malaspina was not quite entirely forgot-

Glasier Bay National Monument, AK

ten. In the St. Elias mountain range in southeastern Alaska, there is a glacier that bears his name. **TS**

MISSING THE BOAT

Captain George Nidever and his crew were sailing their small schooner among the Santa Catalina Islands off the coast of southern California in April 1852. They were looking for seagull eggs, intending to sell them to restaurants — but what they found turned out to be far more interesting.

The captain and some of his crew went ashore at a small island called San Nicolas and proceeded to search for the eggs. Only a few steps inland, they found a surprise: a hut and some poles upon which some seal blubber had been hung to dry. They found small footprints around the hut and began to search for the person who lived there — a woman, they guessed, from the size of the footprints. When a gusty wind sprang up, they had to return to their ship, but Nidever decided he would come back to the island and resume his search for the woman.

Nidever and his men landed on San Nicolas again in May of 1853, this time searching the other end of the island. Soon they came upon a Native American woman, about 50 years old. She smiled and bowed and spoke in a language no one, not even the Native Americans in the crew, could understand. She seemed happy to see other human beings and roasted roots for them for dinner. The crew took her along when they sailed back to Santa Barbara.

Although she was among people entirely different from herself, the woman was able to communicate well through signs. She would often dance and sing ancient Indian chants. Eventually, the mystery of who she was and how she got to the lonely island was solved.

The woman had lived all her life on that island with her people, a tribe of 18 Native Americans. Many years ago, the tribe had been in the process of moving to the mainland when a terrible thing happened. The tribespeople had taken their belongings aboard the ship and prepared to leave their home behind. But the woman suddenly noticed that her own child was not among the group; he had wandered away and had been left on the shore! She insisted that the ship go back to find him, but once she was on the island again a storm blew up out of nowhere, and the ship was forced to leave. The woman and her child were left behind, watching from the shore as the ship sailed away in the crashing waters.

In time, the woman's child died of illness. She lived alone for almost 20 years, eating mainly seal meat and blubber, as well as fish and roots. She passed time making baskets and sewed skin clothing for herself using needles made of bone.

After her rescue, the woman lived for only seven weeks on the mainland. When she died, the fathers of Mission Santa Barbara sent her skin dresses, baskets, needles and other belongings to Rome to be preserved there as historical items. **TS**

DEPUTY SAM IN SILVERBELL

The time was 1904 and the place was the Arizona desert mountains, about 24 miles west of what is now Marana. A copper-mining camp sprouted and grew quickly there, turning into a busy, prosperous frontier town of 3,000 citizens. Those were some of the toughest and most lawless citizens you could find. Perhaps as a joke, someone named the town Silverbell. As tough as it was, though, there were honest citizens living there who wanted to clean it up. And when three men were murdered, the town sent for Deputy Sheriff Sam McEven from Dodge City, who had a reputation as a great peacemaker.

Sam agreed that something had to be done to halt the crime wave that had been overwhelming the town. For weeks he went around persuading most of the miners, ranchers and gamblers to give up their guns. Some men he put in jail; some he fined for carrying concealed weapons. The town settled down quite a bit — until one day Hobie Jackson took a dislike to the Boxer brothers, shooting and killing one of them and badly wounding the other.

A couple of citizens ran to tell Sam about the incident. They told him that Hobie had said he would kill anybody who came after him. In desperation, he had escaped down an old mine tunnel and probably planned to wait until dark and make a run for it then.

Sam strapped on his gun and made his way out to the tunnel. But before he could even give a shout into the darkness, a bullet whizzed past his head. He realized that if he went in, Hobie would see him against the light and be able to shoot him. Sam scratched his head; then he asked his men to bring him a big, heavy ore car and set it on the tracks.

They brought him the car, and Sam began pushing it ahead as he moved into the tunnel. Shots rang out; the bullets clanged on the iron car. Sam just laughed; he continued to drive the killer down a dead-end tunnel. A few minutes later, he walked out with Hobie in handcuffs. It was the beginning of a new, cleaned-up era for Silverbell.

The town didn't last past another two decades, however, and in 1934, after the smelting operations were dismantled in the nearby town of Sasco, Silverbell began to flounder. Today nothing remains but some old concrete foundations and two decrepit cemeteries. **TS**

SWEETGRASS'S
COLORFUL ROOTS

One of the toughest, meanest, bloodiest towns in the entire West helped — in a very odd way — to win a war.

Not all the big gold rushes of the past were to California or Alaska. Montana had some of the yellow stuff, too. Butte, Montana, was the hub of a multimillion-dollar discovery. Wherever a successful claim promised more riches to come — even when that promise wasn't kept — other towns sprung up. Located along the Canadian border in Montana, Sweetgrass was one of those towns. Gambling, drinking and shootings were its main sources of entertainment.

As one old-timer said, "Well, Sweetgrass ain't so much now, but about the time the gold petered out, we had pretty nice little stores, churches, banks, hospitals and stuff like that.

Plus we had a narrow-gauge railroad. Before long we had murders, suicides, and gambling joints as well. But come prohibition, the craziness really started. There were bootleggers all over the place. Actually, it wasn't a very friendly town, considering the number of killings, but we kept going, a few of us, anyhow."

Business picked up, though, in 1939, along with an influx of gamblers, fly-by-nighters and grifters. World War II was getting underway in Europe, and England was in desperate need of fighting planes. The United States had a Neutrality Act that prohibited American or Canadian pilots from flying such planes over the border. So, as the planes were completed by U.S. factories, they were taken to Sweetgrass where crews of workers *pushed* the planes over the line. Then they were picked up by Royal Air Force pilots and flown across the Atlantic to fight the Nazis attacking England.

The town today is a bit more law-abiding than it was. Border patrols on both sides of the line keep wary eyes on smugglers and border-runners. But most of the colorful and overly avaricious characters of its past have gone, and hardly any of them left forwarding addresses. **TS**

Butte, Montana

LOOTED LOGS

Try to imagine a stack of logs 50 feet wide and a sixth of a mile long, floating on the ocean and held together with 175 tons of steel chain. Well, that was the load the lumber schooner *Czarina* was towing along the Pacific coast. Those floating logs would cut up into 5 million board feet of lumber — worth, of course, quite a bit of money.

But one dark night as the *Czarina* was chugging along, the towrope snapped. Remarkably, no one on board noticed.

Next morning, Captain Robertson nearly had a heart attack. He spent two days searching for the missing logs. He was out of luck; not even a twig showed up. He hired two tugboats to search along the coast. There was still no sign of the logs.

The captain pulled at his beard. He knew that by now, those logs should have been carried to the shore by the current and piled up on a beach somewhere, but they hadn't. There was only one explanation: They had been stolen.

Robertson finally cracked the case after one of his crewmen met another sailor in a seaside saloon. The sailor had been fired off the steam schooner *San Pedro* and was not averse to revealing some of its secrets. The *San Pedro*, it seemed, had come upon the huge drifting raft and taken it in tow. The schooner headed south, but the heavy load took a lot of extra fuel. Intending to return to pick up the logs, the skipper anchored his salvage and made for the nearest port for extra fuel.

Captain Robertson chartered a tugboat and when the *San Pedro* left port, he followed. He told his skipper to keep the schooner in sight but to stay well back. Despite his precautions, the schooner's captain spotted him and became suspicious. He changed course.

But Robertson wasn't fooled. He kept right on, due south. And sure enough, he beat his rival in spotting the raft, floating serenely in the sunlight, where it had been anchored for safekeeping. He tied it up and towed it triumphantly back north to the mills it was intended for. History doesn't record it, but chances are good that the dishonest captain of the *San Pedro* never got another shipping assignment again. **TS**

A Logger Next To A Fallen Sequoia

MADAM SUL-TE-WAN

You might have seen her perform in some early silent motion pictures. She was one of the very first African-American artists to find success in films.

Her stage name was Madam Sul-Te-Wan, but her real name was Nellie Conley. She was born in 1874 in Louisville, Kentucky. When she was younger, she worked hard delivering the washing from her mother's laundry business — no one predicted much of a future for her. But as it turns out, she had a lot of talent and also a bit of good fortune. Two of her mother's customers were actresses at Louisville's Buckingham Theater. Seeing the girl's fascination with the stage, they taught her to dance and sing. In no time at all, the young performer was winning competitions. She soon landed the star role of "Creole Nell" in a theatrical company called the Three Black Cloaks.

Africa-Americans always have had a strong role in theater and performance, and during this period, Conley helped form a successful theatrical company of African-American performers and musicians, the Black Four Hundred (which really numbered about 26). After establishing yet another successful theater group, the Rair Black Minstrels, she moved west in 1910 to start a family with her husband. Her marriage was not successful, however, and before long she was looking for work to support her children by herself. She soon found work in the movies.

Conley came on the scene when Hollywood's movie industry was just getting started and was flying by the seat of its pants. Producers in those days were mostly an insensitive lot. They thought pratfalls and pies in the face were high comedy. African-Americans and other ethnic groups were for the most part shown as bad guys or ignorant fools, with a few exceptions. *The Judge's Story*, made in 1911, showed an African-American in a sympathetic role, and so did a film starring Charles Ray titled *The Coward*. But most African-American roles at the time were played by whites wearing black makeup and acting silly.

However, as luck would have it, Conley's timing was excellent: The famed D. W. Griffith was casting for his landmark film, *The Birth of a Nation*, and the word was out that he was looking for African-American actors. Conley applied, and the great director was so impressed that he developed a special scene just for her. Conley's bit *was* terrific, but unfortunately the film wound up extremely long, and her scene ended up unused on the cutting room floor.

She went on to such other films as *The Buccaneer, Mighty Joe Young, Carmen Jones* and others. Her last film appearance was in Sam Goldwyn's *Porgy and Bess*, which was released in 1959. Conley died that same year at the Motion Picture Country Home, at the age of 85. **TS**

ANOTHER KIND OF PRISON

harley Banks was as nice a guy as you'd ever want to meet and awfully smart as well. Although he stole a small fortune from Wells Fargo and Company in 1872, he was never caught — but was imprisoned anyway!

Banks was a handsome and distinguished-looking bank employee. He was a member of San Francisco's most exclusive clubs who owned a library of scientific books and a fine collection of microscope slides. When he failed to show up for work on a Tuesday following a holiday, however, Jim Hume, the former sheriff and the current security chief for Wells Fargo, became suspicious. Hume had the books checked and found a major shortage.

Hume moved quickly. Other Wells Fargo employees told him that Banks had mentioned he would be spending his three-day holiday fishing on the Russian River. Actually though, Banks had sent his wife to New York on a shopping trip and was himself holed up in a local hotel under the name of J. Scard. By the time Hume figured out the ruse, Banks was gone.

While researching the case, Hume discovered that Banks had been living far in excess of his quite-adequate salary. Among other drains on his income was the cost of entertaining three young lady friends, none of whom knew about the others — or about his wife!

Hume, who had nabbed dozens of stagecoach bandits for his employer, was determined to put Banks behind bars. He was delighted when he got word of a package being shipped to a Mr. J. Scard in Rarotonga, one of the Cook Islands in the South Pacific. Hume asked the company attorney to get extradition on Banks. The attorney sadly let him know that the Cook Islands had no extradition treaty with the United States, so there was no way to have Banks arrested and brought back.

Hume thought it over. He figured he would

Jesse And Frank James (seated) With Cole And Bob Younger

not be able to get the money back. "But," he mused to himself, "there's more than one kind of prison."

He had all of the other areas in the South Seas plastered with "Wanted" posters for Banks. If Banks dared leave the Cook Islands, he would be grabbed by local government officials or eager bounty hunters. Hume figured Banks would quickly tire of his South Sea paradise, and he was right. The one-time swinger and swindler was forced to obey strict local law; for instance, he had to be off the streets by 8:00 P.M. His only alternative to following the laws was expulsion from the islands, leading to almost certain arrest.

Because of this situation, Banks led a dull and humdrum life, staying close to home and turning later to religion. He possibly even became honest — for there is no evidence that he ever stole so much as a penny from his last employers. **TS**

THE UNNECESSARY SEAGULLS

uccess tends to be like a prize in a boxing match — you don't always win it in the first round. That certainly was the case for a young man who prepared a particular etching for the U.S. Coast Survey Office in Washington, D.C., in December 1854.

The young man had finished his first year at West Point near the bottom of his class, and in the third year he had been dismissed from the academy for failing to obey the rules. But he did have a keen interest in drawing and mapmaking and a certain skill with an etching needle. His work, like that of the other artists in his department, was to translate survey artists' original drawings onto copper plates. These plates then would be used to print copies of the U.S. coastline for the government's military and maritime activities.

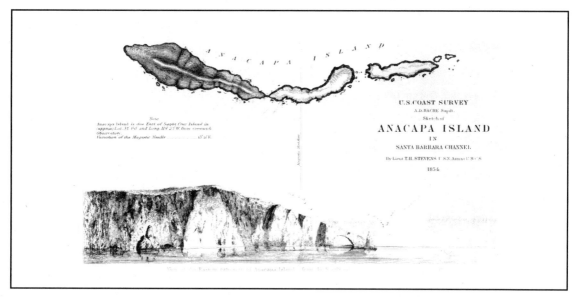

Engraving Of Anacapa Island

The young man started his job on November 7, 1854. The pay was $1.50 per day and the hours were from 9:00 A.M. to 3:00 P.M. However, the pay was never enough to cover his lavish entertainment costs, and the hours were far too long, so he usually showed up late. "I was not late," he would explain to his superiors, "the office opened too early." He even brought in an extra hat and left it at the office when he left early so that others would see the hat and think he was still around.

And yet there were other reasons that the young man's boss in the drafting room, Captain Benham, was displeased with him. It was clear that etching coast scenes bored the young man. Furthermore, Benham didn't approve of the embellishments the young man was prone to add to his etchings — such things as monks, knights and beggars were likely to show up in the margins, and one coastal scene featured sea serpents, mermaids and smiling whales.

Captain Benham would remind the young man of the cost of copper and urged him to focus on his tasks. "James," Captain Benham might have said, "these are for print in official government publications. They aren't supposed to be *beautiful*. Just do the work — and be quick about it!" James' reply was to etch a tiny devil's face on one of the plates, which the Captain came upon with a start when viewing the fine details of the etchings through a magnifying glass.

Captain Benham then gave the artist some preliminary sketches done of Anacapa Island in Santa Barbara Channel off the coast of California. "Get to work," he would have admonished the young man. "And no more of your fancy stuff, understand?"

After the job was finished, however, Captain Benham again found unnecessary additions to the piece. Two small flocks of seagulls hung gracefully in the air above the island's headlands. When criticized for this detail, the young man replied, "Surely the birds don't detract from the sketch. Anacapa Island couldn't really look as blank as that picture did before I added the birds." And so the young artist was dismissed — or he resigned — and his last day was on February 12, 1855.

In the end, however, it turned out to be a good thing. James Whistler left for Paris within a few months, and, by following his true passion, eventually became one of America's foremost artists. The etching he did, "View of the Eastern Extremity of Anacapa Island from the Southward," is known as one of the finest pieces of work that the Coast Survey ever had done. **TS**

CLAM MONEY

The Pomo Indians have been called the "moneyers" of Native Americans because of their elaborate system for trading. Living among the giant redwoods of north-central California, they didn't concern themselves with U.S. currency but focused on what was of value to them, inventing their own kind of money.

The mid-1800s were an interesting time for the Pomos: The Russians were edging in — and so were the Americans. But the local Native Americans and the military men who first moved in got along and did quite a lot of trading. The money that they used was fashioned from shells that they collected, primarily from Bodega Bay. One historical source says that, in the early days of the Pomos' trading with the Americans, the exchange rate was 400 clam shells for $2.50.

To understand how the shells functioned as currency, consider that for a salmon, for example, a Native American might take three "clams," pieces of clamshell polished on sandstone to about the size of a nickel. Shells that had a larger diameter were worth more. The thickness of the shells also influenced their value: The thicker the shell the greater the value. They made bigger deals by using strings of clamshells. After the shells were acquired, they were worn — as pendants, bracelets, necklaces and in other decorative ways. As the shells chafed against one another, they became shinier and therefore more treasured — and more valuable.

The Pomos liked other, harder-to-find shells as well. They prized the soft rock called magnesite. If clam shells were like silver to them then magnesite was their gold. Magnesite was too valuable to the Pomos to be negotiated for on strings; rather, the beads were traded individually. They rubbed the rock down, shaping it into one- to three-inch cylinders, and then they baked it. Heating the rock caused it to turn from a white or gray color to a beautiful pink, red or brown.

Because of the importance the Pomo Indians placed on currency in their trading, they developed a complex arithmetic system; it was necessary for them to be able to accurately count the long strings of polished clamshells. The Pomos' skills ended up being important to their survival.

By the late 1800s, their land was being invaded by ranchers and miners, and they were forced to arrange dealings with the U.S. government that would allow them to buy land. In 1878 one group of Pomo Indians banded together to buy seven acres in Coyote Valley. Later, another group bought 100 acres along Ackerman Creek. Though the Pomos didn't have an economy that meshed directly with the U.S. currency system, their understanding of numbers enabled them to grasp the *concept* of money and to emphasize trading as a method of obtaining as much land as possible. **TS**

SEWARD'S FOLLY

He was gray, bent and weary, and he had served his nation well. But they still called William Seward a fool when, on behalf of the United States, he bought a vast tract of land for two cents an acre.

Russia and the United States were on good terms following the American Civil War. The Russian fleet even had visited New York and San Francisco during the war. America was grateful for this support at a time when most European nations had seemed willing to recognize the Confederacy. Actually Czar Alexander of Russia had freed his serfs about the time Abraham Lincoln freed the American slaves, and there was a feeling of camaraderie between the two countries.

It was then that Secretary of State William Seward decided to take up an old, tentative offer made by Russia in 1854. Russia owned a huge chunk of land along the Pacific side of Canada. The Russian minister to the U. S., Edouard de Stoeckl, had offered to sell the land to the U. S.

Seward had seen the reports of Robert Kennicott, an explorer and naturalist who had been in the far reaches of the Pacific Northwest and the land that Russia owned.

Mount McKinley, AK

Seward thought that the Russians were unaware of the value of their territory. And so he negotiated with de Stoeckl for the purchase. Most of the details concerning the Russian residents of the land were worked out smoothly. The main stick-ing point was the price. How much was a chunk of real estate twice the size of Texas worth?

Seward asked de Stoeckl how much he wanted. The Russian suggested that the land was worth $7 million. Shaking his head sadly, Seward would have negotiated. "Too much, my friend. How about $5 million? No? Then five and a half?"

But the Russian must have sensed how eager Seward was under his cool exterior. "Nyet. It is worth $10 million at least. But in view of the amiable relations between our two countries, we'll accept seven, plus another $200,000 to pay off our outstanding business." With that, the two men shook hands.

The deal wasn't quite so easily settled. It had to be approved by the U.S. Senate by a two-thirds majority. Although Seward lobbied hard to get the approval, many weren't sure, and Seward was in danger of losing. Luckily, Charles Sumner, chairman of the Foreign Relations Committee, came to his aid. Although Sumner had hesitated at first, Seward finally had won him over: Sumner rose and gave a brilliant three-hour speech that turned the tide. The treaty was approved with one vote to spare.

In 1867 Alaska was purchased from Russia. It joined the U. S. as a territory in 1912 and in 1959 became our 49th state, adding immense natural beauty and wealth to the nation. Everyone who thought that Seward was a fool for spending money on this unknown land — well, they were quite simply proved wrong. **TS**

DOCTOR
BETHENIA OWENS-ADAIR

Today they'd call her a super-mom, but back in 1880, when at age 40 she earned her medical degree, all they had to say was, "Shocking!"

Bethenia Owens-Adair was one of nine children who traveled in one of the earliest pioneer wagons into Oregon. She grew into a strong-minded woman. Her marriage at the early age of 14 didn't work out; she was granted a divorce at the age of 18 and returned to her family in Oregon with her two-year-old baby. She could read only a little and could write even less. But she arranged to live with a married friend in return for doing the washing so that she could go to school.

Years later, Owens-Adair would write, "Words can never express my humiliation at having to recite with children from [ages] 8 to 14." By diligently studying, however, she quickly earned her high school diploma — this, she was sure, opened the greatest opportunity of her life.

She found that she had an interest in nursing and volunteered to help the local doctors with their patients. One evening, she was helping out an elderly physician who was trying to perform a simple surgery on a very ill child. Owens-Adair saw at once that the frail man's unsteady hand could cause an injury to his patient. She picked up the surgical instrument and said, "Let me try, Doctor." Before he could reply, Owens-Adair corrected the problem quickly and easily, and the child was instantly relieved. The doctor was furious at her boldness, but Owens-Adair gained new courage from her success.

That episode made the young woman decide to go to medical school. However, she was aware that she would meet with opposition from her friends and family, so she thought about the decision very carefully for an entire year. Meanwhile, she studied medicine in secret, borrowing the medical books of a doctor friend so she could learn enough to prepare for school. When she had the opportunity, she consulted with older women whom she respected. She asked the advice of the great women leaders Abigail Scott Duniway and Susan B. Anthony when they passed through Oregon on national tours, and they both advised her to pursue her dream. By the time the year was over, Owens-Adair had made up her mind. Her family — especially her father — objected to the idea quite strongly, but she was firm.

It wasn't easy for her to find a school that would take a woman, nor was it easy to cope with the prejudices of many of the distinguished instructors. Fortunately, a few of the more enlightened professors helped and encouraged her. She earned her medical degree from the Philadelphia Eclectic School of Medicine in 1872, then went on to receive a post-graduate degree in medicine and surgery from the University of Michigan in June 1880. Later she wrote, "The moment a woman seeks advancement ... she is made the mark of poisoned arrows. It is by her own intrinsic worth and persistent perseverance that she secures a position in any profession."

Owens-Adair enjoyed a large practice for many years in Oregon. Her son and adopted daughter studied medicine as well. In July 1884 she married again — this time happily — and retired many years later, in 1905. Throughout everything Owens-Adair continued to push for the equal rights and equal treatment of women in society. When a lady friend once chastised her for going out in public to treat a patient without wearing a hat, Owens-Adair retorted, "Shall I pause to find my hat when a woman is dying?!" She was truly a woman ahead of her time. **TS**

GAME OVER

In the Old West, gambling was as common as drinking — and just as well regarded. Some states figured those activities were socially unacceptable, and at least made gambling illegal. Despite Nevada's reputation today, with Las Vegas being the casino capital of the country, back in the mid- to late-1800s the state was one of those that followed suit — and outlawed gambling.

In the late 1850s, Nevada was booming with the discovery of gold and silver, and the miners, with their sense of adventure, sought to further their fortunes through games of chance. Nothing changed when Nevada Territory was organized in 1861 and the legislature deemed gambling illegal — the sheriffs were ignored and the laws weren't enforced.

Another anti-gambling law was passed in 1865, but it, too, was ignored. In 1867, recognizing the folly in trying to enforce such gambling restrictions, the legislature tried to repeal. But Governor Blasdel, a Christian with strong convictions, would hear nothing of it and vetoed the bill. After two years of battling, the legislature passed the bill over the governor's veto and gambling once again was permitted openly.

Some 40 years had passed when a group of citizens decided that such activities should indeed be prohibited, and they launched a campaign to stop gambling once again. We can imagine the scene in the back of an unusually jam-packed saloon. (Casinos didn't exist until the 1930s.) Everyone is fighting to get his or her bets down on the gambling tables before the

Gambling Was A Popular Pastime In The Old West

stroke of midnight, when the new law will take effect. Although the air is charged, the dealers seem calmer than they should be. When a regular asks why, the dealer whispers that some places might keep operating for folks they really know.

It was true — even after the law passed, if you knew your way around, you could still lay some loot on a favorite card or number. The back rooms of many saloons were simply ignored by sheriffs. Twenty more years went by — enough time to convince the Nevada lawmakers that they hadn't done right by their golden goose: People still gambled, but the state got no taxes from the underground casinos. The profitable tourist trade had dried up as well. In 1931 the Nevada legislature repealed the anti-gambling law, and in no time at all casinos were booming — this time as a main-street business — bringing in tourists and revenue in what you might call a modern-day silver strike. **TS**

THE GREAT DIAMOND HOAX

Back before jewelers were as skilled as they are today in evaluating the worth of diamonds, two con artists carried out one of the biggest hoaxes of the West — the Great Diamond Hoax.

The time was the 1870s, and the con artists involved were Philip Arnold and John Slack. They were clever and secretive about their business; how they managed to gain an audience with William Ralston, head of the Bank of California, has been lost to history, but somehow they did. Once in his presence, they opened a bag for him to examine — vast quantities of diamonds! They claimed the diamonds were from a hidden mine in Wyoming and that the gems were so thick on the ground that you could scoop them up with a shovel.

Ralston, who'd made his fortune through smart investments, was cautious. He indicated that he might be interested in making some kind of deal. He asked his visitors to leave some of the diamonds so that he could evaluate their worth, and Arnold and Slack agreed.

When Ralston's experts checked the stones and found them to be genuine, the banker moved quickly and quietly. He organized a group of other important financiers throughout California. Before any deals were made, the men asked to see the actual mine. Arnold and Slack once again agreed. Along with Ralston and his engineers, the two con men boarded a train to Wyoming. Arnold and Slack then blindfolded their unwitting prey and led them by a round-about mountain route, ensuring that no one would be able to retrace the way.

Sure enough, at the mine site a gap in the hills sparkled and winked with precious stones. One engineer, Henry Janin, examined the field and reported later that it was worth at least $65 million. Tiffany's in New York examined samples and declared them worth at least $150,000. Ralston and his group offered to pay Arnold and Slack nearly $300,000 for a share in the mine. The deal was agreed upon.

A time came when the financiers were going to sell stock in the mine, and just about then the U.S. government sent a leading geologist, Clarence King, to survey the region. The geologist reported that the mine had been salted — the mine did, indeed, contain diamonds, but only where the land had been disturbed. The mine was worthless; everyone had been duped! A chagrined Ralston paid back his investors out of his own pocket, and that ended the Great Diamond Hoax.

The truth was uncovered over time. Slack and Arnold had traveled to Europe where they bought $50,000 of worthless, low-grade, uncut, diamond discards. Because they knew that jewelers in America wouldn't be familiar with rough, uncut diamonds, they planted them in the mine and plotted their hoax. After having received the final payment for the share of the mine, Slack disappeared and Arnold returned to his native Kentucky. Because of his distance, Arnold escaped California law, but he eventually returned $100,000 to the investors with the understanding that all charges against him would be dropped. Ironically, Arnold himself became a banker in Elizabethtown, Kentucky, where he lived until his death. Slack was never heard from again. **TS**

HOW SEATTLE GOT ITS NAME

he very last thing on earth Chief Seattle wanted was to have an American city named after him, and with perhaps good reason, depending on your point of view.

Chief Seattle was a member of the Suquamish, a small Native American tribe living mainly on Puget Sound. Chief Seattle was kindly and dignified in his older years, but as a young man he impressed the other natives with his force and bravery.

As the leader of his people, it was Chief Seattle's duty to avenge the death of a member of his tribe. When a local Native American medicine man lost a patient, one of Chief Seattle's followers, tribal custom called for the medicine man to pay with his life. Chief Seattle bought a gun at the white man's trading post and shot the medicine man. This act earned him the label of "bad Indian" among the white settlers, who did not understand the native customs.

Chief Seattle's fearlessness was unusual, for his was a peaceable tribe that usually avoided serious conflicts. However, his readiness to fight proved an asset to his tribe. Two nearby tribes, the Haidahs and the Tsimpsians, were warlike. They would burst into the Suquamish settlement whooping and yelling and waving their weapons, scaring the peaceful Native Americans into the woods. Then they plundered all the food and furs. Chief Seattle called a meeting of the Suquamish men and urged them to fight back.

The Suquamish men may have argued that they were not fighters, that the other braves would quickly outfight them, but Chief Seattle had other ideas. "We will fight differently," was his message. He led the men to the river, where the enemy would come in their canoes, and they chopped down a large tree so it fell across the river just around a sharp bend. They waited for the next attack. Soon, the raiders came paddling swiftly down the river. As they rounded the corner —

Chief Seattle

crash! — into the log went their canoes, the warriors falling topsy-turvy into the rushing water. Chief Seattle led his men into the river where they set about the raiders with clubs. The raiders quickly fled, and their medicine man was busy for days patching his wounded warriors.

This victory gave Chief Seattle quite a reputation, and he used his new standing to form a confederation of six neighboring tribes with himself as leader. Chief Seattle never fought against the white settlers, however. He wisely saw that the white man was too large in number to be defeated. In fact, he was even baptized as a Christian and given the name "Noah." The local settlers came to admire him, and, as their settlement began to grow into a real town, they decided to name it after him. To their surprise, Noah declined the honor. "No, you must not," he said. "It is believed the dead awaken when the living speak their names." But his white friends went ahead and named the town Seattle anyway. Now it is one of the great metropolitan hubs of the Northwest. **TS**

A RACE AGAINST TIME

It's 1876 and you've just produced a highly successful run of *Henry V* at Booths Theater in New York. Now what do you do for an encore?

After a great New York season, you'd naturally want to open in San Francisco — a seven-day trip by steam engine. After that, you'd want to tour the country.

Your main problem would be publicity. You'd need lots of it. Henry Jarrett, the company manager for one theater group that performed *Henry V*, came up with the idea of tying in the tour with the biggest development of the day: The steam engine. He came up with an outrageous stunt. The company would not only travel coast-to-coast in luxury, but they would do it in a mere *four days*. Jarrett wanted to set a speed record that would stand for years and would capture the attention and imagination of the public.

The newspapers were full of disbelief.

"Impossible!" they screamed. "The speeds would shake them to pieces. Jarrett's so crazy they should lock him up." But Jarrett just smiled. He told the clamoring reporters that he and the troupe would leave New York after their Wednesday night performance and would open in San Francisco the following Monday.

Jarrett engaged the fastest locomotives of five different railroad lines. He also signed up 16 eager passengers to travel with the company. They received tickets encased in sterling silver covers, a week's room and meals at the Palace Hotel in San Francisco, and, to top it all off, a first-class return to New York. Hundreds of thousands of bets were made on the train's final time.

The evening of May 31, after the company's performance, the passengers boarded the train and it was off, exactly on schedule. The excitement was immense. Great crowds of people gathered at the stations along the way to watch the steam engine roar through. The train made no stops except for fuel and water. The engineers pulled their throttles back all the way, breaking speed record after speed record between the cities. Coming down the Sierra Nevada mountains, the brake shoes wore out, but the engineer still didn't slow down. The train had made it from Ogden, Utah, to Oakland, California (880 miles) in just 25 hours, 45 minutes! It was unheard of in that era.

They reached the Oakland station, where an enormous crowd had gathered to greet them; then they went via the waiting ferry boat to San Francisco. When they got across the bay, hired hacks came to gallop the travelers at full speed to the theater. There they received a 13-gun salute, a speech from the mayor and the cheers of thousands. Ocean to ocean, it had taken them only 83 hours, 59 minutes and 15 seconds — twelve hours *under* Hank Jarrett's original estimate. Needless to say, the theater was jammed to the chandeliers every night for the entire run. **TS**

CHARLIE SAM

They were welcomed at first, these "sojourners" from the Far East who came to work during California's Gold Rush after gold was discovered in 1848. They sent money back to their families in China, and many of them returned home after they had earned enough money — but others kept coming.

By 1880 there were just over 100,000 Chinese people in California, where they were much needed for working in the gold mines as well as in the supporting industries like lumber, fishing, laundries and farming. They worked laying track for the first railroad through the Sierra Nevada mountains, linking California with the East. The work was hard and dangerous; they earned a mere $26 a month for their labor — about what it cost a Central Pacific Railroad contractor for a good work animal and its feed.

Later, however, the Chinese immigrants became targets for political harassment. Once the rails were down and the steam cars were in operation, many jobs disappeared. The Chinese immigrants then had to compete with other Americans for jobs — and the other Americans didn't like that at all. Anti-Chinese agitators like Denis Kearney, an Irish immigrant in San Francisco, instigated fights and riots against the Chinese and called them the "Oriental menace."

Still, some areas of the West were friendly to the much-maligned Chinese immigrants. One of these areas was Yuma, Arizona, a small city located on the Colorado river, which marked the border with California. The Southern Pacific Railroad line extended to Yuma in 1878, and by 1880 it had gone even further into Arizona, all the way to Tucson. Chinese who came with the railroad industry had settled in Yuma and established grocery stores, laundries and other businesses. They had abandoned their traditional style of dress for American clothing, and they worked hard to learn English and establish themselves as Americans — even though an 1868 federal law discriminated against foreign-born Chinese and would not allow them to become naturalized citizens.

It was in Yuma that bright, young Charlie Sam settled after he was hit by the railroad's down-sizing. Charlie had done some mining and trading in claims and had some money. In Yuma, he was able to open a large restaurant which pros-pered.

One evening, a local trouble-maker entered

Chinese Immigrants

the restaurant. He beat up Charlie, as well as an employee who tried to intervene. When Charlie recovered, he found an attorney to file suit against the attacker. The evidence was clear, but the jury in the case couldn't agree on the verdict, and the judge had to dismiss them.

Many people of Yuma were outraged. The *Yuma Sentinel* wrote, "It's a very clear case, but prejudice seems to have played a most important part" in the jury's deci-sion. Charlie called for another trial; this time the judgment was in his favor, and the whole town rejoiced.

In his old age, Charlie returned to his home-land. He left a grandson who attended University of Southern California medical school and became a practicing physician. It wasn't until 1943 that the U.S. Congress granted naturalization rights to foreign-born Chinese. But Charlie often remarked upon how he had found a town in the Wild West where tolerance, not prejudice, won out. **TS**

A HAIRY QUESTION

George Bernard Shaw, the famous (some might say infamous) Irish playwright, critic and commentator, spoke and wrote wittily and caustically about everyone and everything. But when he came west, a cub reporter left him speechless for at least 20 seconds.

In the early 1930s, Shaw came to San Francisco on the ship *Empress of Britain* as the guest of publisher William Randolph Hearst. The long-bearded Shaw held a press conference, where reporters questioned him in depth about his past and about his future plans.

The city editor of the *San Francisco News* had already published a feature article on the distinguished visitor, but he wanted something more. He called in a new reporter named Barron Muller and ordered him to go ask Shaw "a simple, silly question." On the way to the ship where Shaw was packing up, Muller racked his brain. What in blazes should he ask? The young reporter must have been quite apprehensive.

When he got to the ship, Muller was told that Mr. Shaw wasn't seeing any more reporters. Muller wasn't going to be stopped that easily; he made his way through the luxury cabins until he found the noted gentleman's stateroom. He knocked and a crisp voice inside said, "Come." Muller, still trying frantically to think of a question, walked in. As he described it later, Shaw "looked like a shaggy billy goat" and it was that observation that brought the question to his mind. When Shaw told him that the interviews were over, Muller insisted he only had one question to ask.

"What's that?" said Shaw.

"My readers would like to know if you sleep with your beard under the blankets or on top."

Shaw turned red and spluttered; with his face a mask of anger, he ordered the reporter to leave and pushed him out of the stateroom. Muller returned to his editor in despair — he felt he had a story that was no story but wrote it anyway, ending with the question he had asked. When he turned it in, he was probably expecting to be fired for his insolence.

The editor, however, loved the story. It was the beginning of a 40-year career for Muller as a top news reporter. As for what Shaw did with his beard when he slept, that is still a mystery. **TS**

Since they were first organized in 1835, the Texas Rangers have been one of the most efficient — if unorthodox — law enforcement groups in the nation. Its members were tough, quick-thinking and not without a touch of humor.

One superb example is Pinochle Miller, a young Texas Ranger who was caught in a bind and had to do some quick thinking. Miller was deep in Mexico on business involving a mining project. He carried a small camera to take pictures of the type of equipment used by the mining company.

The tiny village where he was staying was nestled in the remote hills — there wasn't a policeman within 200 miles. The village did, however, have a "Revolutionary Army" roaming about which was actually a gang of bandits and Army deserters. This group roared into town one day and captured Miller. Deciding that since he was a foreigner he couldn't be up to any good, they tried him as a spy — a process that took a bit under three minutes. They found him guilty and decided he should be shot at once, in the name of the Revolutionary Army.

The bandits found a clean, white, adobe wall near the cantina in town and backed Miller up against it. While they were milling around, Miller fooled with his camera, setting it up as if to take a picture of the execution. When the camera was set up, Miller lured the leader of the bandits into getting his photo taken. He said something like this: "Captain, this is a very special occasion. I wonder if you wouldn't like to have your picture taken carrying out your duty?"

Apparently the captain thought this was a splendid idea. Miller took shots from several angles. Then he suggested that perhaps the second-in-command would like a picture, too. He certainly would — and so would the rest of the crew. Miller clicked away at groups of singles, doubles and more. The men became more amiable with the flattery. To show that there were no hard feelings, Miller suggested that they should all have a drink. The bandits responded enthusiastically. Miller ordered the cantina to roll out a barrel of *sotol* — a drink made with practically pure strong alcohol.

After a few drinks all around, Miller asked to take some pictures of the men firing their guns. Guns went off everywhere. Several drinks later, the happy army was no longer sure which end of the gun went against their shoulders. And that was when Miller made his move, dashing for the nearest horse, jumping on and galloping away, shouting back, "I'll mail you all the prints."

He would have, too, as a gesture of international good will. The only problem was that during all the picture-taking, Miller hadn't had any film in his camera! **TS**

Photographing Yosemite Valley From Near Glacier Point

THE DOCTOR'S HERD

These days we grumble loudly and often about those sky-high medical costs, and rightly so. How we would have kicked and screamed about doctor fees that were even higher — like the fees a certain doctor charged in California back in the 1840s, before it was even a state.

John Marsh wasn't *exactly* a medical doctor. But he had graduated in 1823 with a bachelor's degree from Harvard University, and he had an impressive nature, a lot of personality and a great bedside manner. He had read books about medicine, and, when he was captured by Indians on the Santa Fe Trail, so the story goes, Marsh

Large Cattle Ranch

had treated the Indians' sick chief thereby saving his own life.

Marsh made it to Los Angeles, arrived on January 1, 1836, and soon convinced the local authorities that he was a legitimate doctor. Since cattle ranching was the largest industry in southern California at the time, Marsh was paid in cow- hides rather than in cash. He sold the hides and moved northward to start a ranch himself. Marsh must have quickly realized his unique position when he got hold of the great Rancho Los Meganos. There wasn't another doctor for hundreds of miles around!

Rancho Los Meganos was a beautiful, fertile, well-watered 70,000-acre tract at the foot of a great mountain — ideal for a cattle ranch. But for a cattle ranch, you needed cattle, and Marsh didn't have any cattle. For that matter, he didn't have any money left either, so he started up his medical practice there, with an eye toward stocking his pastures.

A patient might come to him and say, "Señor Doctor, I have a condition. Sometimes I am hot with fever. Sometimes I have chills." Marsh would respond, "Amigo, you require quinine. That will cost you 25 head of cattle." That was for an office visit, and it was the same for a tonic, a dose of salts or stitches. For a childbirth, he charged 50 head. For an amputation, 100. If he had to go a long distance on a house call, his fee ran much higher.

Dr. Marsh soon owned a tremendously large herd — that meant he had to acquire much more land on which to graze them. In a very short time, he became the first great cattle king of the West Coast.

And he was still the only doctor in town!

THE PALACE AND HER CHEF

There came a time in the late 1800s when, with its booming culture and wealth, San Francisco wanted to do something to show off its grandeur — it did that by building the first luxury hotel of the West: The Palace.

Construction on the Palace hotel was financed by William Ralston of the Bank of California. An enormous, seven-story building, the hotel towered over the city. Located at the corner of New Montgomery and Market Streets, it opened to the public in 1875.

One of the features of the hotel, the Garden Court restaurant, soon became a favorite with the rich and famous. The executive chef, Jules Harder, had had years of experience working in New York's Delmonico's, the Union Club and the Grand Union. He applied his skill at the Palace, offering such food as magnificent ducks, world-famed California oysters, plump quail, venison and abalone – always with fresh vegetables and greens. The cellars were stocked with Europe's and America's finest wines and champagnes. It was a wonderland for an imaginative chef.

The Palace became known as the place for visitors to stay when they came west. Such notables as Presidents Grant, McKinley, Roosevelt and Taft; the Grand Duke Boris of Russia; the king of Hawaii; the millionaires Rockefeller, Carnegie and Pullman– all were guests at the hotel.

While they stayed at the hotel, many of the illustrious dined at the hotel's fabulous restaurant, and Chef Jules judged the visitors based on what they ordered. For instance, President Ulysses Grant's taste improved over the years. The Emperor of Brazil he pegged as a good, plain diner. Alphonse Rothschild he rated tops as he always ordered the finest food.

The Palace Hotel

As for President Hayes? "Ah," said Jules, "President Hayes. I regret that he never drinks wine with his dinners. How can such a man care what he eats?" He added, "The most discouraging experience I have had is to get up something special … and have it make no more impression than a baked potato!" To most of its guests, the Palace hotel made an impression in every regard, however, and the city considered it special — a monument to the ambition and spirit of the pioneers. **TS**

WYOMING WINTERS

The Old West was sometimes hard on its pioneers — but the people that crossed into the new frontier were ambitious and determined and they learned how to survive.

Sam Hicks, who spent his boyhood on a cattle ranch in Wyoming in the 1880s, wrote about the challenges his family faced surviving the bitter cold of winter. Up around the Hoback River, where Hicks grew up, ranchers had to cope with temperatures around 50 degrees below zero — considerably colder than a modern freezer. Getting ready for the winter was a major job for the Hicks family, especially because their spread was 43 miles from the nearest town.

Hicks describes their preparation for the looming winter: "While the roads were still open, Dad always trucked in two tons of flour and a couple of 50-pound cans of lard, buckets of coffee, two or three big sacks of sugar, and some feed sacks full of dry beans. Also, we packed in a ton of potatoes, 500 pounds of carrots, bushels of apples, cases of canned corn, peas and tomatoes." The family packed these supplies in an underground cellar, with kerosene lamps left burning to keep the food from freezing.

Hicks reported, "In addition, Dad used to kill eight or ten head of elk during December. We quartered the meat and stored it in a shed, where it froze solid." The family always kept an elk quarter thawing out behind the kitchen stove. When it thawed, they could peel back the hide and cut off enough steak to feed the family and any company that dropped by.

The Hicks family was quite large — thus the need for so much food. In addition, their farm was centrally located, and people were always stopping in on their way to somewhere else. Hicks wrote, "Mother never knew 10 minutes before mealtime whether she would have the regular family of eight for supper, or a crowd of hungry hay diggers, timber men and trappers.

And when neighbors stopped in, they'd usually spend the night as well, with an early morning breakfast of elk steak, biscuits and gravy to fuel them on their travels."

Today's ranchers live a slightly different lifestyle. They have special machinery for breaking through the snow and motorized toboggans to deliver hay to the feed grounds. But one thing hasn't changed for Wyoming ranchers — they still have to be prepared for those cold, endless-seeming winters. **TS**

GREAT GRAPES

Count Agoston Haraszthy was a human dynamo, an eternal optimist who created a whole new industry in northern California.

Haraszthy might have lived his life peacefully farming on his family estate in Hungary. But he and the Hungarian government had different ideas about how the country should be run; as a result, he was forced to leave the country before the police arrived at his door.

At the age of 28, he hit America like a hurricane. In 1840, in the rolling hillsides of Wisconsin, Haraszthy planted vineyards and founded a winery. Eventually, though, he decided it was time to move on.

Haraszthy had heard of the gold rush of 1849, and he decided that he, too, would go west — but not for gold. His research convinced him that California had the ideal climate for wine grapes. At first he tried growing in the hills south of San Francisco, but it was too foggy. So in 1858, he moved on to a large acreage in the sunny Sonoma Valley.

Haraszthy had managed to find the right soil and the right climate, but he did not find the California grapes to his liking. In 1861, Haraszthy was asked by California Gov. John Downey to go back to his native lands and gather samples of European grapes, and he gladly accepted the task. In search of the right plants, he and his son traveled throughout Europe, collecting choice cuttings of such varieties as Riesling, Zinfandel and Emperor grapes. They brought back more than 100,000 cuttings to the Golden State, planting many and distributing others to their friends. This time, the harvested grapes were as fine as the very best in the world.

Each season, Haraszthy entertained the elite

Making Wine At The Buena Vista Winery

of Sonoma at his vineyard, where he built a reconstruction of a Pompeian Villa and held balls. On October 23, 1864, the first formal celebration of winemaking in California was marked by a masquerade ball; the guests of honor were General and Mrs. Mariano Vallejo. Haraszthy and Vallejo often competed at state fairs to see whose wine was the best. It's a good bet that Haraszthy won many of those competitions. And with California wine-making off to such an inspired start, it was only a matter of time before it would become a major industry.

Haraszthy's careful selection and skilled growing techniques earned him the title "Father of California Wines." His vineyards in Sonoma Valley are still in operation and are known as Buena Vista Winery. Thanks to his great start, today all over the surrounding northern California countryside other vineyards and wineries are thriving. **TS**

OREGON SUFFRAGE

The great and lovely state of Oregon would have gotten woman's suffrage sooner or later. Due to a very determined homemaker and mother, though, it got the vote sooner.

Abigail Jane Scott was 17 when she and her family trudged 2,400 miles from Illinois to French Prairie, Oregon. The trip took almost six months of walking past hostile Pawnees, through raging rivers and over lonely mountains. Abigail kept a diary of events on the trip, including her mother's death. When she finally reached Oregon, she found relatives who gladly welcomed her and her father, brothers and sisters.

Abigail applied for a schoolteacher's job and was accepted — fortunately, no one in the 1850s bothered with official credentials, because Abigail had none. She did, however, have a quick mind, a flair for the written word, and a deep conviction that when men spoke of themselves as "protectors of women" they really meant "exploiters." At age 18, she married amiable young Benjamin Charles Duniway, but only after they agreed to leave the word "obey" out of the wedding vows.

Benjamin wholeheartedly agreed that women weren't getting a fair deal. He told Abigail that he thought things wouldn't improve until women were allowed to vote. "Someday a woman will start something," he said — not knowing that that woman would be Abigail. Shortly thereafter, Abigail visited San Francisco and encountered the first suffrage newspaper in the West. Returning home, she told her husband that she wanted to start a paper, too.

Abigail was a success: Not only was she a talented writer, it turned out, but she was a top-notch editor as well. She knew that readers would be intrigued by controversy and charmed by humor, and so she gave them both. The *New Northwest* paper did well. Later on she would publish an autobiography (called *Path Breaking*), two novels and some poetry. To support her cause, Abigail also went on tour. Once she encountered a heckler who said, "Me and my dad, we have always been against women voting." To which Abigail replied, "My mom and I

Women Signing Up To Vote

always believed the difference between a man and a mule is that a man can change his mind." Another time she asked a small boy at the edge of her audience, "Sonny, don't you think your mother, who cannot vote, is as good as a Salem saloon bum, who can?" The embarrassed boy answered, "Sure, I guess so — I mean, um, she's better!"

As the years passed, Abigail and her followers lost one referendum after another, but they persisted. Finally, when Abigail was 78, Oregon granted women the right to vote. Abigail was the first woman to vote in the next election, in 1914.

In a ceremony to celebrate suffrage, Governor West told Abigail, "You know, Mrs. Duniway, I've been an admirer of yours for a long, long time." Abigail smiled. "How long would that be?" she asked. Some say that the governor replied, "Ever since I was a small boy and you asked me if I considered my mother as good as a saloon bum!" **TS**

A TOAST TO TETRAZZINI

A world-famous singer and a powerful theatrical producer had a fearsome fight in the first decade of the 20th century. The winner was the city of San Francisco, which had just risen from the ashes of the 1906 earthquake to become the "Paris of the Pacific."

Oscar Hammerstein, the great American producer, owned and operated theaters all across America. Luisa Tetrazzini was known around the world for her glorious soprano voice. She was especially loved in San Francisco, where she had made her American debut in 1904. The two famous people made a deal: Hammerstein agreed to pay Tetrazzini a salary higher than any other singer had ever received. In return, Tetrazzini had to agree never to sing in any theater except those owned by Hammerstein.

Tetrazzini was so enchanted with San Francisco, however, that she told reporters she would sing for its residents even though there were no Hammerstein theaters in town. Everyone was overjoyed at the news — everyone except Hammerstein. He was furious. He told Tetrazzini she was absolutely *not* to sing in any other theater — and he took out a court order to hold Tetrazzini to her contract.

The dispute made newspapers

Lotta's Fountain, San Francisco

around the world. Because of her feud with Hammerstein, no other theater manager in San Francisco dared to engage her. But Madame

Tetrazzini was very determined, and, as she had promised, she *did* sing in San Francisco on Christmas Eve in 1910. She wore a trailing white gown, a broad-brimmed hat, white gloves and a white ostrich boa.

She didn't break her contract, though — she didn't sing in a theater at all! She sang at the corner of Third and Market Streets, at Lotta's Fountain. It was one of her finest concerts, and when she sang "Auld Lang Syne" as a finale, a quarter of a million voices joined her. **TS**

LUCKY IKE

The man who always wore the black hat and black bow tie believed in luck. He also had a rather high opinion of himself. It seems possible that Ike Pryor was right on both points.

Ike's early years were full of hardship, but he was as persistent — and some say as obstinate — as any westerner alive. He was stingy, too. Born in Tampa, Florida, in June of 1852 and all but orphaned as a boy, Ike was a rich man by middle age from dealing in land and cattle.

Ike was the kind of guy who'd look over a large chunk of property out in the West Texas brush country, pick it up for $1.40 an acre, and in just a few years it would be worth a couple of million. One time he sold a piece of land to a buyer for an enormous profit and got a large down payment. But the payment drained the buyer's accounts, and the man's luck ran short. When he defaulted on the rest of the payments, Ike took the property back. After that, gas was discovered under Ike's land – millions of dollars right there underground.

Ike didn't gamble much on cards or dice, but one tale tells of a trip to Mexico City with one of his friends, a professional gambler. They visited several clubs, but Ike didn't lay any money down. When they came to the richest club in the city, Ike's friend told him, "Ike, if you're going to bet at all, here is your last chance." So Ike put one silver dollar on a roulette number and won $18. When he bet using his new winnings, he won even more money. He just kept betting and winning. Ike's friend got nervous when he saw that Ike had such a huge pile of chips in front of him. He nudged Ike and recommended that he cash in.

"Not yet," Ike said, "I'm going to win three hundred more."

He bet the bank and won $300. By now, any normal person's luck would have run out. But not Ike's. The next day there was a raffle for a huge diamond ring. Ike bought a $5 ticket and won the ring. He gave it to his wife when he returned home, and she wore it for as long as she lived.

He may have had more than his share of good luck, but the fact is that Ike was a sharp thinker, too. As the Spanish-American War began in 1898, he arranged for a man in Cuba to keep him informed of events. He learned that the U.S. naval blockade on Cuba would be lifted as soon as the surrender was signed, and Ike figured that the Cubans would need new supplies very quickly. He made arrangements for ships to move his cattle to Havana; he paid $5 per head for his ship-

Ike Pryor

ment of cattle and cleared about $80 per head once the beef was sold in the Cuban markets.

For a time, Ike was the president of the most important two associations of cattle ranchers in the United States, and he even entertained the notion of running for governor of Texas. It's unclear why he never did, but no doubt he would have done well at that too, for his statement, "I've always been a winner," *was* true, if somewhat immodest.

Ike was 85 years old when he died in 1937. It's quite possible that he'd raised, bought and shipped as much cattle as anyone in the world — and that's nothing to beef about. **TS**

THE TALKATIVE TRAVELER

When we think of people who lived and worked on the frontier, we generally think of direct and practical folk who were economical with words and didn't care for extra talk. Often the jabbering newcomers who came by the freshly opened railroads got on the nerves of the Western folk.

Johnny Dunn was a stagecoach driver in New Mexico, running the route between the town of Taos and the nearest railroad line. The route was through rough mountains and deep canyons, up steep grades and around tight corners. But if Dunn's typical Western passengers felt any fear or trepidation, they held their tongues about it.

The Easterners, however, were a different story. On one particular afternoon, Dunn picked up three passengers at the train junction and set off for Taos. The passengers were two men and one woman who had probably just arrived from the East, as there weren't a whole lot of women in the West in those days. It was quite a ride!

According to those who know the story, the two men didn't say one word between them, but the woman could hardly contain herself. At the frightful mountain drop-offs, she gasped, "Oh, my!" And no doubt at every new vista came an "Ooooooooh!" from her lips. As the stagecoach careened down the hills, she pleaded with Dunn, "Oh, do be careful!"

Finally they reached the stage stop in Taos, outside one of the town's grander hotels, and the white-faced passengers disembarked. The first man asked, "How much?"

"Two and a half," came the reply. The man handed Dunn a fiver and waited for his change before going off to the business at hand. Then the next man paid for the ride, took his luggage and said good-bye. Last of all was the woman, who also handed Dunn a five dollar bill. He put it in his pocket and proceeded to mount the stagecoach.

"Aren't you going to give me my change?" asked the woman.

"You don't have any change coming that I know of," was Dunn's reply.

"But you charged those men only two and a half apiece," she protested.

"Yes, I did," Dunn replied. "But you see, *they* didn't *talk*." **TS**

A Typical Stagecoach, 1860s

DOUGLAS FIRS

He was a rotten little kid — sullen, cantankerous and stubborn. But David Douglas turned out to be a first-rate explorer and botanist who left his name on one of the West's most prolific and profitable trees.

Douglas was born in Scone, Scotland, in the early 1800s. Even his parents couldn't stand seven-year-old David; to get him out of the house, his stonemason father and his mother sent him to the home of a Scotch nobleman who was a gardener. The young boy was to be an apprentice, and surprisingly he turned out to be a wonder at growing rare tropical plants. He also had the opportunity to read all the botany books he could get his hands on.

At the end of his 10-year apprenticeship, Douglas got a job at the Horticultural Society of London. In 1823, the society sent him to eastern North America to collect samples of fruit trees. They were delighted with what he brought back and they sent him out again, this time to western North America.

Douglas sailed up the Columbia River on a Hudson's Bay Company ship, reaching Fort Vancouver. There, he seems to have fallen in love — with a plant. He encountered the shrub called *salal*, which had been described by an earlier explorer. Douglas wrote, "So pleased was I that I could scarcely see anything but it." But still he collected seeds of the sugar pine and other specimens and returned to London. In all, he had spent over 10 years exploring more than 7,000 miles of rough terrain through drenching rains and freezing winds.

Back in England, Douglas was taken up by high society, but he didn't really fit in. He was a loner with few social graces, and he eventually asked his employers to send him back to North America, which they gladly did.

By that time, much had changed in America. More Europeans had moved to the once-wild places, and the formerly friendly Native Americans had become hostile. On this trip, Douglas sailed to California. He wasn't much impressed, however. He reported that all anyone seemed to do was drink wine and ride horses. Also, he didn't like the weather, with its short botanical season. That year, he collected only 500 species. He was ill by then, worn out by hardship, and his eyes were going bad. He went on to the Sandwich Islands to continue collecting, and that was where he eventually died, in 1834.

His name lives on, though — some of the seeds he took back to England grew into handsome trees, which the Horticultural Society named the Douglas fir in his honor. Decorated with tinsel, ornaments and gifts, they are favored as Christmas trees — a cheery legacy that plain, sulky David Douglas might not have fully appreciated. **TS**

WHY THE COWBOYS SANG

Trail bosses aren't in very big demand these days. But if you should ever find yourself having to drive a herd of 3,000 cows 1,000 miles or so, you'll want to know why the cowboys sang.

Western movies show cattle running across the plains, herded by pistol-shooting riders, but that wasn't the way it was really done. In the Old West of the 1880s, running a steer was bad business because the stress and speed involved caused the animal to lose weight, making it worth less at the market where it was to be sold.

Most of the time cattle arrived at the railhead in prime condition, and an expert trail boss knew it was his job to keep the cattle in such shape. To make sure his animals grazed, drank and traveled in a content frame of mind, he'd quietly organize their approaches to a river or water hole a few at a time. A distraction —

Cowboy, 1870's

someone on a nervous, high-spirited horse, for instance — had to be kept away from the herd. For if the herd panicked, the cattle would run, losing hundreds of pounds in a very short time.

It took a bit of cow-sense, too, to be a good cow man. You'd learn that you didn't have to run your horse crazy trying to bring back a runaway calf: The calf would eventually come back on its own for dinner. And when some of the full-grown animals broke off and ran, you'd just let them go, because they'd quickly tire and lie down of their own accord.

Those trail bosses mainly ambled their cows along at a slow, easy walk. If they were old-timers, they'd sing to them, too. The songs had to be suitable for their pace, and so slow, sad songs mostly fit the bill. Favorites included "Oh Beat the Drum Slowly and Play the Fife Lowly" and "Bury Me Not on the Lone Prairie." Sometimes as the cows plodded along calmly, the cowboys even sang hymns to them. **TS**

THE GREEDY CUSTOMS COLLECTOR

Victor Smith was probably the only American ever to threaten naval bombardment of a western town, and he intended to fire his guns from the *Shubrick*, a U.S. government ship, no less.

Smith was a close friend of Salmon P. Chase. Chase was Abraham Lincoln's secretary of state who later became chief justice of the U.S. Supreme Court. Chase appointed Smith customs collector at Port Townsend, in Washington Territory. It was a tiny but very important job — the entire settlement existed mainly for the purpose of collecting customs fees from importers who unloaded their ships there.

Smith not only had a talent for doing everything wrong, but he also managed to anger everyone in the area. One of the first things he decided to do was move the customs house from

Port Townsend to Port Angeles. The residents of Port Townsend were furious, but Smith explained to Secretary Chase that the move was to obtain a better harbor. He neglected to mention that he'd recently bought a large tract of land in Port Angeles, or that the value of his property would skyrocket because of the move.

Then Smith made a giant mistake. He decided to go to Washington, D.C., for a while, and he called upon Lieutenant Merryman of the U.S. Revenue Service to stand in for him. The conscientious lieutenant reviewed the office records and found that the absent customs collector had been using his powerful position to collect funds for his own benefit. He reported the fraud to Secretary Chase.

Smith soon learned the news, and he rushed back to the port, ordering Merryman to hand over the incriminating records. But Merryman refused. Smith was enraged. He threatened to instruct the commander of the *Shubrick* to shell the customs house. The lieutenant realized Smith was desperate and might do as he threatened, endangering the residents. So he handed over the records, and Smith left on the cutter. The furious townspeople ordered an arrest warrant, but Chase ordered that the charges be dropped.

Was it a clean getaway? Not quite. Smith first went to Washington, D.C. Then he supposedly left for San Francisco, carrying a large bag full of millions in currency and bonds. The ship was wrecked; Smith survived, but the portmanteau was lost. When Smith boarded another ship, the *Brother Jonathan*, bound for Puget Sound, this ship also sank. This time, Smith went with it. **TS**

A RISKY CROSSING

Her name was magic anywhere in the world a hundred years ago. Sarah Bernhardt was surely one of the greatest and most daring actresses on any stage. She made and lost fortunes as often as she married and divorced — and at one point she even gambled her life and the lives of her crew.

It was a blustery winter when Bernhardt and her entourage headed west by rail. On February 6, 1881, she was riding a special train of three cars carrying her and the entire troupe of performers, musicians and backstage hands on their way to New Orleans. There had been unusually heavy rain, and flood waters had risen. Because the railroad bridge over St. Louis Bay appeared ready to collapse, Bernhardt's train was stopped. When the engineer was reluctant to continue, Bernhardt insisted.

At first the engineer could not believe she was serious, but Bernhardt wouldn't budge. Finally he told her he would run the train on one condition: Before they began the crossing, Bernhardt had to give him $2,500, which he would immediately send to his wife. If they crossed safely, he would see that it was refunded to her; if not, it would go to help his widow. Bernhardt agreed. "I had a vision of the responsibility I had taken upon myself," she later wrote, "for it was risking without their consent the lives of 27 persons."

With steam up and whistle blowing, then, they started across. Water was within inches of the rails. The engineer sped across the flimsy structure as quickly as he could, while the theater folk clung to one another in terror. Bernhardt stood erect and smiling; if she was afraid, she would not let it show. When they were safely on the other side, the passengers shouted for joy. A moment later, the bridge behind them collapsed and sank into the muddy waters!

Bernhardt told the engineer to keep the money, but her conscience, as she later wrote, "was by no means tranquil and for a long time my sleep was disturbed by the most frightful nightmares." So, we can imagine, was the sleep of the 27 people whose lives she had gambled to get to her engagement on time. **TS**

Sarah Bernhardt

THE LAND OF FUSANG

In the year A.D. 499, Emperor Wu Ti of China granted audience to an old Buddhist monk. If the emperor had taken action on the incredible tales he heard from the monk, the continent of America would probably be known today as "Fusang."

The old monk was named Hui Shen, and he had just returned from a 40-year voyage. He had sailed north from China, almost always keeping in sight of land. As far as can be determined, he made his way past the Bering Straits, along the shores of what are now Alaska, British Columbia, Washington, Oregon and California and down the coast of Mexico. He and his comrades settled in what is now Acapulco. When he finally returned to China to report on his adventures, he dictated a history of his experiences — a record that has survived to this day in the 230th volume of the *Great Chinese Encyclopedia*, which was compiled by Chinese historians between A.D. 502 and A.D. 556.

In the audience chamber of the emperor, Hui Shen recounted what he had seen. "Your Majesty," he said, "we sailed 7,000 miles to a land of many marvels. In this land, the people could read and write. They had no fortresses or walled cities, no weapons of war or soldiers. They never made war against each other."

The emperor asked, "And these gifts you bring me, 300 pounds of silk and this mirror, a foot in diameter, made from a single black gem? Do these come from this land?"

The monk replied, "They do; the silk is from a tree called Fusang, and the black gem is born in a fiery mountain. Also, a little over 300 miles inland from this strange land is another marvel: A land of women. In this land, the females are covered in hair, walk erect, and chatter constantly among themselves. They bring forth their babies in only six or seven months, and these babies are fully grown in three or four years." Hui Shen had many more tales of the newfound lands, and the Emperor ordered the court historians to record them all.

Is it really possible Hui Shen discovered America 10 centuries before Columbus? The theory has quite a bit going for it. For starters, the distances recorded by Hui Shen on his voyage are amazingly accurate. The "silk" could have been a cloth still made in Mexico – not from silkworms but from a tree called the maguey or century plant. The chattering "females" he spoke of are almost certainly Central American monkeys, which are much larger than most monkeys found in Asia. And the gem-like mirror could only have been obsidian, a kind of volcanic glass common to the fiery, volcanic regions of Mexico.

As with so many events long gone, it's hard to get historians to agree on anything. Most, however, are on the side of Hui Shen, and some archeological finds support them. Someday we'll know more — and then perhaps we'll celebrate Hui Shen Day, instead of Columbus Day, in honor of the first discovery of America. **TS**

YELLOW BIRD, THE NOVELIST

You might have heard the story about Joaquin Murieta and his gang — one of the most feared bands of outlaws in the Old West. They terrorized and murdered people as they rampaged California, robbing miners, raiding houses and holding up stage coaches. Their reign of horror came to an end in the mid-1800s when a posse organized by a man named Harry Love caught up with the bandits.

As evidence and to collect the reward for Murieta's capture, the posse cut off Murieta's head and the hand of his cohort known as "Three Fingered Jake." The head was preserved in a jar of alcohol and displayed at local fairs where it could be viewed for a small fee. But stories have a way of taking on a life of their own, and many people say that a great deal of the Joaquin Murieta story never really happened, that fact and fiction grew together — much of Murieta's evil reputation is said to have come from Yellow Bird's novel.

The novel was entitled *The Life and Adventures of Joaquin Murieta*, and its author was mysteriously credited only as "Yellow Bird." Yellow Bird was John Rollin Ridge, a Cherokee Indian who earned his living writing and editing in the West.

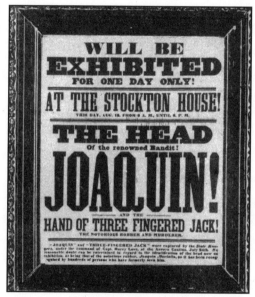

Poster Announcing An Exhibit Of Joaquin's Head

His book on Murieta may have been the first novel written by a Native American author. Like the villain in his novel, Ridge had his own share of adventure in his life — albeit a different sort of adventure.

Ridge's father was one of the Cherokees who favored the government's removal of the tribe to the Far West. Such politics didn't sit well with the other members of the tribe, and they murdered Ridge's father in cold blood, right in front of young John. Ridge vowed revenge against the killers, but he was greatly outnumbered.

Deciding to remake his life, Ridge and his wife traveled to California, where Ridge wrote and edited for the *Marysville National Democrat* and the *San Francisco Evening Journal* newspapers. He also contributed often to the literary magazine, *The Golden Era*. Ridge used the pen name Yellow Bird, a translation of his Cherokee name, Chees-quat-a-law-ny. In 1854 his book about Murieta was published. "I expected to have made a great deal of money off of my book," Ridge is recorded as having said. "And my publishers, after selling 7,000 copies and putting the money in their pockets, fled, busted up . . . and left me with a hundred others, to whistle for our money!"

Ridge was determined to find success, however. And he wanted to make a difference in doing so. He proposed to set up a Native American newspaper that would be a way "not only of defending Indian rights and making oppressors tremble, but of preserving the memories of the distinguished men of the race . . . [and] the most important events of Indian history."

On February 3, 1857, Ridge published the first issue of the *Sacramento Daily Bee*. From the beginning, the newspaper focused on democracy, freedom and the future of Native Americans. Ridge eventually left Sacramento and sold the *Daily Bee,* but he continued his career, editing and owning newspapers throughout California — all of which promoted Native American politics and revealed a piece of Ridge's own strong soul.

TS

ONE GOOD TURN

Sometimes cities can be rivals — like San Francisco and Los Angeles, which snarl at each other even though they're 400 miles apart. In 1889, Seattle and Tacoma were in the same kind of rivalry — until June of that year, when everything changed.

Chicago's famous fire had Mrs. O'Leary's cow to blame. In Seattle, it was a glue pot in a carpenter's shop that boiled over and set the city ablaze. The fire broke out around 2:30 P.M. on June 6, 1889, while Josiah Collins, the chief of the volunteer firefighters, was on a business trip in San Francisco, California. Because most of the structures were made of wood, the fire spread rapidly from building to building. But Collins's firemen knew their jobs. The problem was that there just weren't enough of them — or enough of the fire engines, either. An hour after it started, the blaze was still roaring.

Firefighters Racing To A Fire

Just at its worst, though, the firefighters heard a great clanging and rattling through the smoke. A great red fire engine came roaring to their aid — on its side, the gold lettering "Tacoma Fire Department" was blazoned.

Other cities sent help, too. Firefighters came from Port Townsend and Snohomish and New Watcom and other northwestern cities and towns. In the end, 64 acres of Seattle's business district were burned out. The loss was estimated to be between $12 and $16 million. The *Post Intelligencer* building was destroyed and so was the *Seattle Times* building. A few small-job presses were still operating, though, and they managed to get out miniature editions of the papers. The Madison Avenue cable car resumed service, running cautiously down the hill to the point where the fire's heat had warped the rails.

Not surprisingly, much of the inter-city animosity disappeared. Some time later, when legislators tried to take the state capital title away from Olympia, Seattle remembered that city's aid and returned the favor by throwing their voters against the move — on the theory, no doubt, that one good turn really *does* deserve another. **TS**

A PICTURE OF THE OLD WEST

One of the most important photographers of the West was Evelyn Cameron (called Eve by her friends), who was born on a country estate in England in 1894. Eve and her husband, who was an ornithologist by trade, came to eastern Montana to try their luck at raising polo ponies. The venture failed. Her husband, Ewen, was in favor of packing up and heading back to England, but Eve wanted to stay; despite the hard winters and work, she enjoyed the rough lifestyle.

They stayed and, to supplement their scant income, Eve got out her camera — one of the very few around at that time. She sold her photographs to ranchers, cowboys, storekeepers and neighbors. Eve's work was far more than mere snapshots. She had an artist's eye, and her fine portraits captured the hardy spirit of the settlers around her. She documented the awesome buttes and prairies of the unsettled Montana badlands. And she helped to record information about the birds that her husband knew so much about, especially birds of prey like eagles and hawks.

Her photos alone would have ensured Eve's position as an important historian, but there was more. She kept diaries, several volumes in fact. A sample entry reads: "Arose at 6:50. Fire on. Milked. Breakfast 8:15. Swept, washed up. Took setting hen off eggs. Watered 3 foals. Carted manure from old corral; took down 6 loads before lunch at 2:15. Worked until 7:45. Supper 8:15. Thin beaten steak, mince, poached eggs, rice, tomatoes, coffee, pears."

After Eve died in 1928, her diaries and photographic plates gathered dust in a relative's basement. Fortunately, a woman named Donna Lucy discovered them. She edited the material and put it all in a book, entitled *Photographing Montana: The Life and Work of Evelyn Cameron.* The book is a compelling and inspiring tribute to a woman who surely never dreamed that the record she made of her life and the lives around her would someday become a historical treasure.

TS

WILD HORSES

Think of the Old West and chances are you think of cattle roundups like the ones portrayed so often in movies or on TV. But Westerners also held another kind of roundup that few people have heard of.

One of the most exciting — and dangerous — jobs of the early *vaqueros* or cowboys was to round up wild horses. Young Pedro Villegas' father owned a ranchero in a remote part of California. One day in 1851, furhunters told him of the bands of very fine wild horses living in the shade of the Cascade Mountains to the north. Pedro, his father and his father's men decided to make a trip to capture some of these small, tough animals and bring them back home to breed with their own stock. After several days, the *vaqueros* were close enough to the bands to get into position without being detected. They stationed a pair of men every two or three miles

Corralling Horses

along the valley for about 20 miles.

No doubt Pedro wondered how his father planned to catch the wild horses, which were scattered in small bands all through the great valley. The question was soon answered, however, when his father ordered his men to ride straight at the first herd. The men rushed forward on their mounts with whoops and shouts, and the startled herd took off at once, thundering away down the valley. The men chased this group toward the next group of horses, which also took off. Then the men steered this larger group toward the next band. Soon the tiny, scattered bands of horses had melded into one large herd.

Though the soil was grassy, the hundreds of hooves soon raised a huge cloud of dust. The noise was like nothing young Pedro had ever heard before. The mad race picked up; at each two-mile station, another pair of *vaqueros* joined the chase, whooping and shouting. The frightened horses ran even faster.

After three hours, the *vaqueros* managed to edge closer to the exhausted horses. The *vaqueros* twirled their lassoes and threw, and each throw stopped another wild horse. The *vaquero* quickly tied the horse's legs so it could no longer run and then went about lassoing the other horses.

For Pedro, sitting that night with the *vaqueros*, laughing, talking and singing by the campfire, it had been the most exciting day of his life.

TS

BURNT COFFEE

When disaster strikes, you never know who might — or might not — come to your aid. Sometimes help comes from the most unexpected places.

Back in 1906, the Brandenstein brothers were just getting started in a coffee, tea and rice company in San Francisco. They worked hard, were well-liked in the trade, and were getting a growing number of small orders. Then, one April morning, the whole city of San Francisco started to shake, and then to burn.

Afterward, Manfred Brandenstein picked his way to what had been their warehouse and office. All around him lay ruined buildings — the *Chronicle* Building, the Claus Spreckels Building, the famed Palace Hotel. The Brandenstein Building itself was a smoking ruin. Manfred's brother had gotten there ahead of him. You can imagine the conversation the brothers must have had. "It's all gone, Manfred! Tea and coffee sacks burned, our records in ashes, even the iron safe with our accounting notes crashed three stories down and burst open. There's nothing left."

"We were doing so well, too." Manfred replied. "Just four days ago we got that big order from the Kamakowa brothers in Fresno. That money alone would have refinanced us, but we can't fill it now. There's no way we can meet the delivery date."

The situation *was* grim. All the banks were closed. The Brandensteins tried borrowing from friends and family; most were sympathetic, but few could help. When all was said and done, the brothers raised only enough to open a temporary office. Their position was perilous: Without more business, they would have to close up again.

A few days later, the Brandenstein brothers received a telegram. It read, "Please accept $14,000 advance payment for our recent order.

We will wait. Being from Japan, we understand earthquakes." It was signed, "Kamakowa brothers, Fresno."

With that advance payment the business was saved. From then on it prospered, and today it produces such well-known products as MJB coffee — a brand that wouldn't exist if it weren't for a sympathetic customer. **TS**

BEN HUR MEETS LINCOLN COUNTY

In western movies, there was often a bad guy who owned most of the land in the county and made life miserable for the honest ranchers there. That is, until the good guy came along to straighten things out. In the 1870s in New Mexico, it happened for real. They called it the Lincoln County War.

The chief villain in this drama was named Larry Murphy. He ran a general store and controlled all the cattle ranching, farming and other business for miles around. You couldn't get a job, buy land, or just plain *exist* if Murphy didn't like you. If you didn't pass muster in his book, it was quite likely that one of his goons would sidle up to you and growl something like, "Stranger, there's a stage outta' here at five o'clock. See that you're on it." Ordinary citizens obeyed without question, fearing a visit

Lincoln County Courthouse

from Murphy's hoodlums.

One day a man named McSween, a minister-turned-lawyer who never touched liquor or firearms, started a bank in Lincoln County. Then he opened a store that greatly undercut Murphy's outrageous prices. To no one's surprise, Murphy didn't take much of a liking to McSween. Murphy's posse shot McSween's young Englishman partner — killed him in cold blood.

McSween had a backing among the townsfolk by that time, though, and his followers began shooting, too. When Murphy managed to trap his enemy and many of his followers, he killed them. But that didn't end matters — the survivors on both sides kept shooting.

At this point, President Rutherford B. Hayes had heard about what was going on. He removed Governor Axtell of New Mexico, who couldn't or wouldn't take steps to stop the fighting. Then he called in General Lew Wallace, a hero of the Civil War. Wallace at first declined the job of restoring peace to Lincoln County. He wanted to finish a book he was writing. The president, however, pressed him and at last he agreed.

When Wallace arrived in Lincoln County, the war seemed destined to continue until every last man was dead. But Wallace knew what needed to be done. First he talked with everyone on both sides of the issue. He then declared an amnesty for those who would testify in court and promise to abide by the law. Gradually, Wallace brought the area under lawful control. Peace was restored, and Wallace became the hero of another — if much smaller — war.

Then Wallace went home and finished writing his book, which he called *Ben Hur*. It became a runaway best-seller for years and later was the inspiration for two major Hollywood films. **TS**

SHARPSHOOTER IN A DRESS

She was a small lady, only five feet tall, with a pretty face and a big smile. She also had an eye that made her the greatest shot in the world. Her name was Phoebe Anne Oakley Mozee — later she renamed herself Annie Oakley.

Annie was born in 1860 to a poor family in the Ohio backwoods. As a child, she yearned to escape poverty, and she began to hunt and trap in the north country woods, selling her game to a grocery store. In order to give the animals a fairer chance, Annie always took her shot when the rabbits or grouse were on the move. Even hunting this way, she made enough money to pay off the mortgage on her mother's house.

How did she become such a crack shot? She offered these words of wisdom: "You must have your mind, your nerve and everything in harmony. Don't look at your gun. Simply follow the object at the end of it, as if the tip of the barrel was the point of your finger."

In those days, exhibition shooting was as popular as rock concerts are today. Competition was fierce — and one of the top competitors was Frank Butler, a good-looking, friendly-natured young man of 21. Someone once dared him, "Frank, there's an unknown over at Greenville that some folks are willing to back against you for $100 a side." Frank laughed, "Sure, any time. I can use the money."

Little did Butler know that the "unknown" was small Annie Oakley. Years later he recounted, "I almost dropped dead when a little, slim girl in short dresses stepped out to the mark with me — and never did a person make more impossible shots than did that little girl. She shot 23; I shot 21. It was her first big match and my first defeat."

The two shooters may have been competitors professionally, but personally it was a different story. They eventually married and Frank became her manager. They did well together:

Annie Oakley

Annie took on Europe and beat some of its greatest shooters. From 1885 to 1902, Annie was the main attraction in Buffalo Bill's Wild West Show, where she performed such stunts as shooting a dime in midair or shooting the edge of a playing card. By 1915 Annie and Frank were comfortably retired. Annie volunteered to give exhibitions to soldiers in training for World War I, and she continued demonstrating until the Armistice in 1918. Six years later, she was injured in an automobile accident and did little shooting afterward. Her health gradually declined and she died in November of 1926. Eighteen days later, Frank died as well — of old age, some said, although it was quite plain that he really died of loneliness. **TS**

INDEX